NOMAD

MATT GAMBLE THRILLER SERIES BOOK 3

GARY WINSTON BROWN

This is a work of fiction. Names, characters, places, and incidents – and their usage for storytelling purposes – are crafted for the singular purpose of fictional entertainment and no absolute truths shall be derived from the information contained within. Locales, businesses, companies, events, government institutions, law enforcement agencies and private or educational institutions are used for atmospheric, entertainment and fictional purposes only. Furthermore, any resemblance or reference to persons living or dead is used fictitiously for atmospheric, entertainment and fictional purposes.

This book is dedicated to my beautiful wife, Fiona.
I'm lucky to have you in my life and in my corner.

ILYBBOBKS...ATS

PROLOGUE

Nest 5

H YESAN, NORTH KOREA
Reconnaissance General Bureau 37 (RGB 37)
Organic Warfare Research & Containment
Nest 5, BSL-4

DR. SOO PARK, chief research scientist at RGB 37's biosafety level 4 containment lab, listened as the inflated bladder of Nest 5's airlock door released its compressed air. The hissing sound subsided. The wheel located at the center of the lab's submarine-style door spun, stopped, unlocked. The warning light above it turned from red to green. An alarm sounded as the door opened. Her colleague, Dr. Jin Cho, entered the room, locked the door behind her. The alarm stopped; the lock light turned red. The room was sealed airtight once again.

Soo looked up from her microscope. "Well?" she asked. "What did they say?"

Jin crossed the lab, seated herself at her workstation beside her fellow researcher, placed a file folder on the desk between them. Aware of the many security cameras and omnidirectional microphones placed throughout the room, some in plain view, others not, Jin spoke quietly. "It's confirmed. We leave for Vladivostok soon."

"So, it's really happening," Soo said.

Jin nodded. "It is."

There had been rumors. A delegation of North Korean scientists was being vetted by a secret group whose membership occupied the highest ranks of military and political power within their government. The selected individuals would be attending a meeting in the Russian port city located northeast of their border.

Soo stared into the microscope's eyepiece, adjusted the dials. "Why us?" she whispered.

"Why do you think?" Jin replied quietly. "Because it was our Nest that developed Synoxin-9."

There were ten labs, or nests, located within the clandestine OWRC facility. Nest 5 had made the most progress on the assignment. All Nests had been tasked with developing a potent, pressurized nerve agent capable of being housed within the nose cone of a nuclear warhead, long-range missile, or attack drone. Upon impact with the intended target, or if detonated remotely while still in flight, the organic compound within the nose cone would be released into the air. The agent, a nanoparticulate, had been specifically formulated to propagate upon contact with air and begin to feed on the surrounding oxygen, instantly converting it to carbon dioxide. Every living creature within the proximity of its ever-expanding cloud would be asphyxiated. Death would follow, which was the intent. Synoxin-9 had the ability to wipe out an entire city, or country. Drs. Park and Cho had further developed a failsafe for the nerve agent which made it intelligent and controllable. With the press of a button, the expanding nano cloud could be turned off and rendered inert or turned back on and reactivated, giving their government the unprecedented ability to strategically manage the geographic extent of the cloud's destruction. Now, Synoxin-9 was in the hands of a ruthless dictator who believed the world had underestimated his country for far too long.

To make matters worse, Russia had agreed to the establishment of a military alliance between the two countries. The goal was simple. Under their joint control, a new world order would be formed, one which their adversaries wouldn't see coming until it was too late.

"We should never have developed this," Soo whispered.

"I know," Jin agreed. "But we have. The damage has been done. There's nothing we can do about it now."

Directly above the women, a camera whirred within its round, plastic housing.

They were being observed.

Soo stood, slid her stool under the table, rolled her shoulders, massaged them. The camera followed her as she crossed the room to the supply closet. She removed a box of alcohol cleaning wipes, returned to her workstation, wiped clean her microscope eyepiece and lens. The camera above her made no noise. Whoever had been observing her was no longer interested in what she was doing. "What's in the folder?" she asked.

Jin opened the folder, removed two sheets of paper, handed one to Soo. "Our itinerary," she said.

Soo read the information as she wiped down her equipment. "We're delivering the keynote?"

Jin nodded. "To our Russian counterparts."

"I don't understand," Soo said. "We're sharing our research with them?"

"Don't question this, Soo," Jin replied. "Just attend the meeting and do what's being asked of you."

"I know, but…"

Jin's tone turned sharp. "Do you love your son like I love my daughter?"

Soo was taken aback by the comment. "What kind of question is that? Of course I do."

"Then fall in line. You don't want to go home and find Tam gone, or worse. That's what will happen if you make waves. Do I have to remind you about what you told me two months ago?"

Soo sighed. "No, you don't."

"Then we understand each other?"

Soo nodded. "We do."

She thought about her younger brother and how he had told her of his plans to escape the country. For weeks he had trained in the Sea of Japan, swimming up and down the coast of Wonsan, staying close to the shoreline so as not to arouse the suspicion of the armed guards who patrolled both the beach and the waters, building up his endurance in the process, and becoming a daily fixture in the area. He had informed his sister that he had even made friends with several of the sentries. Late one afternoon, he put his plan into action. When the time was right, he dove beneath the surface and began swimming underwater as far as he could, rolled on his back, surfaced long enough to take a gulp of air, then dove again. After enduring the swim for twelve hours, he broke the surface, utterly exhausted. A small fishing boat plucked him out of the South Korean waters north of Gangneung. He received medical attention and was later provided with refugee status in the country. At last, he was free. He had told her that one day he would find a way to help her escape, but never having heard from him again, she did not know if he was dead or alive.

Soo brought her hand to her neck, played with the charm which hung from her necklace. It had been a gift from her brother, a tiny gold dolphin.

For a moment, she allowed herself to dream about being as free as the magnificent sea creature.

The camera above her whirred again. Instantly, the sound of the surveillance device shattered the fantasy.

She dismissed the thought of freedom and returned to work.

SOO AND JIN listened to the end of day prerecorded announcement of thanks from the Supreme Leader as it was broadcast through the ceiling speakers. They had thirty minutes in which to wrap up their work, leave the lab, change, and meet up with the rest of the scientific staff at the transportation rally point beneath the lab.

Soo whispered to Jin as she changed into her street clothes. "Are you ready to present our findings in Vladivostok?"

Jin nodded. "As I'll ever be."

"Are you worried?"

"About?"

"Going to Russia."

Jin shrugged. "Should I be?"

"I don't trust them," Soo said.

Jin nodded. "No one trusts the Russians."

"I can't put it into words," Soo said. "Something about this trip feels... off."

Jin laced up her running shoes, slipped on her jacket. "You're giving it too much thought. They're not interested in us personally. Only our research."

"What if they decide to keep us there?"

"You mean *kidnap* us?"

Soo nodded.

Jin shook her head. "That would never happen."

"Why not?"

"Our supreme leader would never allow it."

"He might."

Jin raised a finger to her lips. "Shh," she said. "That kind of talk will get you killed."

"Are you going to tell your family about the trip?" Soo asked.

"Absolutely not," Jin said. "I never discuss my work with anyone, especially my family. Besides, this trip is secret."

"But you'll be away for days."

"I'll tell them I've been instructed to stay onsite for an indeterminate period of time. That will be enough. I won't elaborate any more than that, nor would they expect me to. You'd be wise to do the same."

Soo said nothing.

Jin paused. "Please tell me you don't tell your mother about what we do here."

"Very little."

Jin's reply carried with it a hint of anger. "Are you out of your mind? You know the RGB keeps tabs on us even when we're not in the lab, right?"

Soo nodded. "I suspect they do."

"*Suspect*? You can count on it. Don't tell your mother anything ever again!"

"It's hard not to. I have no one else to talk to since..."

"Did Soek know?"

The memory of Soo's late husband and the accident that killed him quieted her. "Yes, he did."

Jin shook her head. "You should never have done that."

"You don't suspect..."

Jin whispered. "Soek was struck and killed in broad daylight by a government vehicle while walking along the side of the road. You were told there were no witnesses, right?"

"That's right."

"And you were told the name of the road on which he was struck?"

"Yes."

"Everyone knows that road. It divides two parcels of farmland. That area is worked every day by dozens of farm workers. The RGB told you the truck that hit him had encountered a mechanical malfunction, lost control, veered off the road and struck him. Right?"

Soo nodded.

"Don't you find that the least bit suspicious? You and I both know Soek's accident was no coincidence."

"Are you saying he was killed because of something I told him?"

A nervous expression crossed Jin's face. "I'm not saying another word about this, and neither should you."

A ten-minute warning alarm sounded. The women closed their lockers, left the change room, took the elevator down one floor to the pedestrian passageway, walked to the bus pickup station, waited. Minutes later, the bus arrived at the stop. As Jin and Soo boarded the bus, an armed RGB officer handed them a black hood. No instructions were necessary. They knew what to do with it, as did every passenger that followed them onto the bus. The women took their seats. Soo sat beside the blacked-out window, placed the hood over her head. Jin did the same. They would not be permitted to remove them until the bus had delivered them to their homes.

They had been working at Nest 5 for the past two years, yet neither of them had any idea where it was located.

Forty-five minutes later, the bus slowed to a stop. The front door opened. The officer called out. "Dr. Soo Park."

Soo stood, walked to the front of the bus, removed her hood, handed it to the officer, disembarked. She watched as the bus drove down the street and disappeared around the corner.

She was home.

1

Pretty Blonde

R

IGGER'S WATERSPORTS
Christ Church, Barbados

MATT AND KYLA walked through the lobby of the Casuarina Beach Hotel, entered the outdoor restaurant, then waited for the server to escort them to their table. Matt seated himself across from Kyla, kept the parasailing, scuba diving, and watercraft rental shack in sight. He watched as the crew of the converted tugboat *REEF EXPLORER* tossed empty scuba tanks overboard, jumped into the warm aquamarine water to retrieve them as they bobbed in the gentle surf, then carried them up the beach to the watersports shack.

Kyla turned in her chair, glanced at the boat and its crew. "You see him?" she asked.

The waiter returned to the table, informed them of the restaurant's afternoon special: Bajan flying fish, served with macaroni pie and coleslaw. Matt accepted the recommendation. "We'll both have the special," he said. "And two glasses of water, please."

"Of course, sir," the waiter replied. "Right away."

Matt perused the beach, the dive boat and its departing customers, answered Kyla. "Not yet."

"Are you sure this is the spot?"

Matt nodded. "If TFC Cross says this is where we'll find Morris, then yes, this is the spot."

Kyla smiled. "You know, we could mix a little pleasure with business later today if you'd like."

"What did you have in mind?"

"A trip into the city."

"What are you looking for in Bridgetown?"

"Colombian Emeralds."

"The store?"

"It's not just a store. It's *Colombian Emeralds*. We could pick up a little something."

"For me?" Matt smiled. "Thanks, but emeralds aren't my thing. I'm more of a Rolex guy."

"Very funny."

"Oh, something for *you*."

"Yes, for me," Kyla said. "Unless you were planning on buying something for your *other* girlfriend."

Matt shook his head. "I can't afford another girlfriend. Case in point? This discussion."

"You're in charge of NOMAD, Matt. Task Force Chief

Cross gave you an unlimited budget. You can purchase anything you require, right?"

"Yes, but I don't think that privilege extends to buying emerald jewelry for my girlfriend."

Kyla pouted playfully. "Your spring is wound a little tight. You know that?"

Matt pointed to the Rolex Cosmograph Daytona watch he wore on his wrist and smiled. "Like a fine Swiss timepiece." He lowered his sunglasses, glanced at the man who had just ascended from the galley, watched him as he leaned over the boat railing and talked to his deckhand, who was busy wrangling scuba tanks in the water below. "Got him," he said.

"Where?"

"On deck."

"What do you want to do?"

"Hold."

"Why?"

"I want to see who's with him."

"You're expecting someone else?"

"I am. Our number four, Julia Shore."

Kyla stared at Matt. "That name sounds familiar."

Matt nodded. "I've mentioned her before. She's responsible for me leaving my professorship at Baylor and being recruited by the agency."

"Of course," Kyla replied. "I remember her now. She set you up."

Matt nodded. "Yes, she did."

"I suppose I should thank her for that. If she hadn't, we'd never have met."

"You'll be able to do that in a few minutes."

Kyla turned in her seat, caught sight of the pretty blonde

as she stood. She had been suntanning on the front deck of the boat, lying out of sight. Kyla turned back, stared at Matt. "That's her?"

Matt nodded. "Mm-hmm."

Kyla turned back, glared at Matt. "If you think I'm going to let you work with someone that gorgeous, you're out of your mind."

Matt smiled. "It's a sacrifice I'm willing to make in the interest of national security." He stood. "Wait here. I'll be right back."

Matt left the table, found the waiter, spoke to him briefly, tipped and overpaid for the meal, then returned to the table. "Come on," he said. "Time to meet the rest of the team."

"What about lunch?" Kyla asked. "I'm hungry."

"I'll make it up to you later," Matt replied.

As Matt and Kyla exited the restaurant and walked along the beach towards the watersports shack, the waiter seated an elderly couple at their former table. The two perused the menu, whispered, then stood to leave.

The waiter returned, spoke to them. "Is something wrong?" he asked.

The woman tried to hide her embarrassment. "We're sorry," she said. "You have a beautiful restaurant here, but we're afraid the prices are above our budget. We're sorry to have bothered you."

The waiter smiled. "Not today they're not."

"Excuse me?" the man said.

The waiter pointed to the table. "Please," he said. "Make yourselves comfortable."

Curious, the couple returned to the table. "I don't understand," the woman said.

"Do you like flying fish with macaroni pie and coleslaw?" the waiter asked.

The woman smiled. "It's my favorite Bajan meal. Bert's too."

Her husband nodded.

"Then you visited us on the perfect day at the perfect time," the waiter said.

"Why is that?" Bert asked.

The waiter pointed to Matt and Kyla as they walked along the beach. "The gentleman saw you arrive. He offered to pay for your meals: either the special or anything else you would prefer."

The woman looked shocked. "That's never happened to us before," she said. "I don't know what to say. Thank you."

The waiter smiled. "No worries. Your meals will be right out. Enjoy."

As Matt walked toward the watersports shack, he glanced over his shoulder, saw the woman looking at him.

She waved.

Matt nodded, waved back.

2

Rigor Mortis

MATT LEANED AGAINST the wall of Rigger's Watersports and watched the crew carry the last two tanks up from the beach to the beachfront business. Kyla sat at a nearby picnic table, protected from the scorching sun by a large red and white beach umbrella which promoted Banks beer, an island brew popular with locals and visitors alike. The big man Matt had been surveilling from his table at the restaurant jumped into the water, waited until his bikini-clad companion joined him at the stern of the boat, then helped her down from the swim platform into the warm water. The pair made their way to the shore. The woman looked up toward the scuba shack, saw Matt standing there. She paused, then let out a joyous shriek. "Matt! Oh my God, *Matt!*"

Julia Shore ran up the beach to Matt. He stepped away from the shack and caught her as she ran into his arms.

Matt laughed and accepted her huge hug. "Hi, Julia," he said. "Good to see you again."

The big man reached the scuba shack, spoke to Matt. "Wish I could say the same."

Matt extended his hand. "How are you, Roger?"

Roger shook it. "I was fine until I saw you, Gamble."

Matt smiled. "Still holding a grudge?"

"My ribs remembered you first."

"Right," Matt said. "You'll have to remind me. How many did I break? Was it three or four?"

"Four, asshole."

Matt shrugged. "You should have blocked."

"I would have if I'd had a chance."

Matt smiled.

Julia stepped back, took Matt's face in her hands and smiled. "You're still as handsome as ever."

Kyla looked up at Matt from the table, cleared her throat.

Matt got the message, introduced her as she stood. "Julia, this is my girlfriend, Kyla Reese. Kyla, Julia Shore."

The women smiled and shook hands.

"You're a very lucky lady, Kyla," Julia said. "There wasn't a female student at Baylor who didn't want to get Professor Gamble between the sheets. Looks like you've achieved the impossible."

"I consider it one of my life's greatest accomplishments," Kyla replied.

"What are you doing here, Gamble?" Roger asked. "We saw the Alpha One Priority. I thought you'd be dead by now."

"The Alpha One was a misunderstanding," Matt replied. "No harm done."

"Cancelling a capture/kill order never happens," Rigor replied. "That directive had to come from Cross himself."

"It did."

"Did he send you here?"

Matt hesitated. "In a manner of speaking."

Roger sighed. "Look, Gamble. It's been a long day. I've had to keep my eyes on eight amateur divers who get wet maybe four times a year if they're lucky, and each one thinks they're Jacques Cousteau. All I want right now is a hot shower and a cold Banks and not necessarily in that order. So do me a favor and fess up."

Kyla spoke to Matt. "Is he always this abrupt?"

Matt smiled. "Kyla, meet Roger Morris. Or as he's known in the agency, Rigor."

"Rigor?"

"As in Rigor Mortis."

"Ah, I get it," Kyla replied. "Roger Morris... *Rigor Mortis*. Clever." She turned to Rigor. "Did you come up with that on your own, or did you have help?"

Rigor chuffed. "Your girlfriend is cute, Gamble."

"Yes, she is," Matt replied. "And yes, we're here because of Cross."

"What does he want with me?"

"Not just you. Julia, too."

"Neither of us received an agency directive. We haven't for a while. Our services aren't in demand in the Caribbean."

"They are now."

"Says who?"

"Me."

"You're not high enough up the food chain to issue orders, buckaroo."

"On the contrary, water boy. That's exactly what I'm here to do."

"You serious?"

"Couldn't be more."

Rigor shook his head. "Son of a bitch."

"I suggest you two shower up and change," Matt said. "We have a lot to discuss."

"Are we going to like what you have to say?"

"Does it matter?"

Rigor sighed. "I suppose not. Where and when?"

"There's a restaurant up the coast in Speightstown called Goddard's. It's on the water. You know it?"

Julia nodded. "I do."

"It's quiet and out of the way," Matt said. "I'll fill you in over dinner. How's seven?"

"We'll be there," Rigor replied.

"Good," Matt said. "See you then."

3

Questions

MATT AND KYLA arrived at Goddard's restaurant fifteen minutes early and were shown to a seaside table in front of a stone breakwater. The Caribbean Sea rolled into the rocky shoreline, deflected off the wall, and sent a gentle mist rising into the air. Underwater lights integrated into the bottom of the winding stone structure shone brightly out into the sea, their beams fading the farther out they stretched into the dark water. Matt and Kyla looked over the wall and watched a mother sea turtle and her two babies slowly swim past, their majestic bodies illuminated by the bright lights, then turned away and vanished into the blackness of the sea. As quickly as they had appeared, they were gone.

"Beautiful creatures, aren't they?" Kyla asked.

Matt nodded. "They are."

"I have a question for you, Matt."

"Shoot."

"What was that earlier about breaking Rigor's ribs?"

"It couldn't be avoided," Matt replied. "I didn't know he was an agency operative at the time, or that Julia was either."

"What happened?"

"I was teaching a self-defense class at Baylor in my off-hours. Nothing too extreme, just a few basic Krav Maga techniques which my students could employ to incapacitate an attacker should the situation ever call for it. Julia was one of my students. Rigor and another guy tried to attack us while I was walking her back to her dorm room. She'd told me she suspected she was being stalked and that she didn't feel comfortable walking back to her room alone. I told her I'd be happy to accompany her. We were almost at her building when a van pulled up and two guys jumped out. One of them was Rigor. They came at us hard and fast. One of the guys picked up Julia and tried to force her into the van. There was no way I was going to let that happen. I lost it. Rigor got hold of me, tried to choke me out. I broke the hold, locked his elbow, then went to work on his ribs. When I felt his body go limp, I knew he wasn't a problem anymore, so I went after the other guy. He let go of Julia, pulled a knife, then looked at Rigor. He must have changed his mind about trying to use the knife when he saw the shape Rigor was in. I delivered a spinning back kick to his face, which knocked him to the ground, but he scrambled to his feet and took off with Rigor hot on his heels. The two of them jumped into the van and took off. It had no plates, so it would have been impossible to track down. Besides, at that time, I was more concerned about making sure that Julia was all right than chasing them down."

"That was the setup you talked about."

Matt nodded. "Ferriman showed me Rigor's picture and that of the second attacker when he and Julia approached me two days later. He was her handler at the time. They revealed the truth about what had happened, told me who they worked for, and that the attack had been an agency exercise. Ferriman told me I'd broken four of Rigor's ribs and the other guy's nose."

"The second guy got off lucky."

Matt nodded.

Kyla looked toward the restaurant's reception desk. "Your guests of honor have arrived."

The pair stood as Rigor and Julia made their way to the table.

"Gotta hand it to you, Gamble," Rigor said as he looked over the breakwater and took in the beautiful view. "You have great taste in restaurants."

Matt and Kyla took their seats. "Goddard's is one of my favorites," Matt replied.

"I take it you've been to Barbados before?"

"I own a place down here."

"Where?"

"Royal Westmoreland Estate."

"So, you knew we were here."

Matt shook his head. "I had no idea. That info came from Cross."

The waiter arrived at the table, handed them their menus, then excused himself while they perused the offerings.

"Order whatever you want," Matt said. "It's on the agency."

Rigor set down his menu, stared at Matt. "What's going on, Gamble?" he asked.

"What are you talking about?" Matt replied.

"You show up out of nowhere, tell us Cross provided you with our cover location and exactly where to find us, which, as you know, is classified information, and you expect me not to have questions?"

"So ask."

"For starters, why are you two still alive? The last Alpha One Priority message Jules and I received pertaining to the two of you was an agency-wide capture/kill order. It was rescinded two days after it was issued. That just doesn't happen with a CKO."

"The answer to that is above your pay grade, Rigor."

"Bullshit."

"All you need to know is that you and Jules have been reassigned. You work for me now."

Rigor leaned back in his chair, stared at Matt. "I think I see the problem."

"There's a problem?"

"Yeah."

"What's that?"

"Somewhere between leaving my dive shack and arriving here, you struck your head. Might been a falling coconut, or maybe you slipped and whacked your head on the pavement. Whatever happened, it scrambled your brain. Go home, take an aspirin, and get a good night's sleep. By morning, you'll be thinking straight." Rigor stood to leave. "Work for you, my ass." He turned to Julia, held out his hand. "Come on, Jules," he said. "We're out of here."

"Sit down," Matt replied firmly.

Rigor ignored the request. "If you think Ferriman would assign us to work for a guy who one month ago was considered persona non grata by the agency, you're delirious."

"Ferriman knows nothing about this or that we're even here. This directive comes from TFC Cross himself, and maybe one higher power."

"And that would be?"

"God."

Rigor stared at Matt, then took his seat. "All right," he said. "I'm listening."

4

Kind of Catchy

"ARE YOU TELLING me that out of all the operatives in the agency, Task Force Chief Cross picked us to work with you?" Rigor asked.

Matt shook his head. "No. Cross gave me the autonomy to assemble a team of my choosing and one month in which to do it. I told him I wanted Kyla, you, Julia, and no one else, which is why you're sitting across from me right now."

"Why us, Matt?" Julia asked.

"Because I like your style," Matt replied. "I'm not an easy person to deceive. I see through most people quickly, yet I never suspected that you were anyone other than the university student you presented yourself to be. I figure if you could pull the wool over my eyes as convincingly as you did, you'll be able to do it to anyone else. I need a person with that kind of ability. A chameleon, if you will. Someone who can insert themselves into any situation and not arouse suspicion. Kyla shares that skill set with you. You two would work well together. That, and everything else I learned about you after reviewing your agency file. Rigor's too."

Rigor leaned forward. "How the hell did you get access to our…"

Matt removed his cell phone, called up the file he needed, cut him off mid-sentence. "Julia Avery Shore. Daughter of the late Allan Shore, noted chemical engineer and former CEO of Applied Life Sciences, a multibillion-dollar scientific research firm. Your father was also involved in an off-the-books, military research project for the Defense Advanced Research Projects Agency, which no one at ALS knew about."

"What are you talking about?" Julia replied. "My father never worked for DARPA."

"He did," Matt replied. "The project was codenamed Channeler. It was run by a scientist by the name of Dr. Jason Merrick. Your father consulted on Channeler. All the file said was that there were complications with Merrick's research and that the project was terminated."

"He never spoke about it," Julia said.

"He couldn't. It was top secret. Had he done so, DARPA would have sent him to prison and tossed away the key. Which brings me to your upbringing. You were educated all over the world. In your youth, your family traveled extensively because of your father's work as an industry consultant prior to starting Applied Life Sciences. You have a gift for languages and dialects. Besides English, you speak five languages fluently, namely French, Spanish, Korean, Russian, and German." Matt smiled. "Apparently you totally faked me out at Baylor since it says here you hold black belts in taekwondo and hapkido. Like me, you're a certified pilot, scuba diver, and parachutist. You came to the attention of the agency after successfully hacking into the computer system of a CIA cover company, which you thought was a legitimate organization. They didn't take too kindly to that, so they went after you, found you, and limited your options to being prosecuted by the agency or going to work for them. Thankfully, you chose the latter."

"Is there anything you don't know about me?" Julia quipped. "My bra size, perhaps?"

Kyla smiled. "36C?"

Julia rolled her eyes. "Cute."

Kyla spied the waiter approaching their table from across the terrace. She raised her hand, splayed her fingers: *five more minutes.*

The waiter nodded, then turned his attention to his other guests.

Matt continued. "Which brings me to Roger Morris, more commonly known in the agency as Rigor Mortis, or by his codename, the Coroner."

"You're the Coroner?" Kyla exclaimed. She leaned back in her chair. "Holy crap. You're a friggin' legend!"

Matt continued. "More field kills than any other operative in the agency. Specialist in close-quarters combat." Matt smiled, winked at Rigor. "Although after our little dance at Baylor, you might want to brush up on those skills."

"You got lucky," Rigor replied. "You were being tested, remember? Trust me, if the directive had been to take you out, we wouldn't be having this conversation right now. You'd be six feet under."

"Maybe," Matt replied. "Maybe not."

Rigor smiled. "Any time you think you're up for a rematch, say the word."

The conversation was becoming heated. Kyla interjected. "Okay, boys. Dial it back. Matt, continue."

"Yeah, Gamble," Rigor said. "Continue. This ought to be interesting."

Matt read Rigor's file on his phone. "Came to the agency by way of U.S. Naval Special Warfare and Operations. Served in the Middle East for two years as a SEAL with Delta Platoon, Team Three. Expert sniper. Medal of Honor recipient. Forced to leave the teams after you tore your meniscus carrying a fellow SEAL to safety who had been hit while under enemy fire, then eliminated the threat by taking out the insurgent who'd shot him. Were it not for that act of bravery, he would have died then and there. You wanted to be a team guy more than anything, but when your injury didn't heal properly that was off the table. Bad for the Navy, good for us. Your record was exemplary. In addition to expertise in CQC, you're a PADI Divemaster, expert off-trail navigator, mountaineer, free climber, parachutist, wingsuit base jumper, improvised weapons and demolitions specialist, and you can fix just about anything with an engine. It also says here you're an accomplished chef. That last one doesn't quite fit the resume."

Rigor crossed his arms. "Cooking helps me relax."

Matt smiled. "Ever consider knitting?"

"Funny."

Matt paused while the waiter returned to the table and took their orders.

"So, what exactly does Cross want from us?" Rigor asked.

"I've been tasked with assembling a black ops team, one that will operate completely off-the-books," Matt replied. "I report to him tomorrow to confirm my team. I had the entire agency to choose from. I chose you three."

"Lucky us," Rigor replied as the waiter delivered their drinks to the table. He nosed the Scotch, rotated the glass, inspected the legs as they ran down the inner wall of the tumbler, took a sip, nodded approvingly. "Nice," he said.

"What will this team be responsible for?" Julia asked.

"Anything and everything," Matt replied. "We go anywhere in the world that we're needed."

"What about agency support?" Rigor asked.

"We'll have a direct line to Cross and his contacts. Other than that, we're on our own. Which is why your individual talents are so important. They have to be enough to get us out of any situation we might find ourselves in."

"And if we can't?"

"Then Cross will see to it that we get four stars engraved on the Memorial Wall at Langley."

"Well, that's something."

"What do we do about our covers, Matt?" Julia asked. "Rigger's Water Sports is well known on Dover Beach. We have regulars. We can't just close it down."

"On the contrary," Matt said. "Nothing changes where your covers are concerned. You have people who work on the boat with you. Train them to manage the operation while you're away. Tell them you want to do a little traveling while you're still young enough to enjoy it. They'll buy that. The agency has a cover business just north of Grantley Adams International Airport. We'll be using it as our base of operations. Here's the address." Matt handed Rigor and Julia his cover business card. "Yours are waiting for you at the company," he said.

Rigor accepted the card, read the business name aloud. "Global Confectioners. We're in the candy business?"

Matt nodded. "Chocolates. It keeps it simple. If asked what you do, being in the candy business requires little explanation. Everyone knows what it is."

"Smart," Rigor replied. "This sounds better every minute." He smiled. "To be honest, I could do with a change of scenery. Don't get me wrong, I love this island. But even beach life can get a little boring. Did Cross give this group a name?"

Matt nodded. "He did. NOMAD. Non-Official Mission Asset Deployment."

Rigor repeated the name. "Nomad. That's kind of catchy."

"I thought so too," Matt said. He raised his glass. "To NOMAD."

Matt, Kyla, Rigor, and Jules accepted the toast, clinked their glasses together. "To NOMAD," they said.

The CIA's newest international covert team was born.

5

Global Confectioners

G LOBAL CONFECTIONERS
(CIA cover platform)
Charnocks, Christ Church, Barbados

THE FOLLOWING MORNING, Matt and Kyla entered
the lobby of Global Confectioners, a gourmet chocolate
manufacturing company located in Charnocks, just north of
Grantley Adams International Airport. Giselle Kingsley, the
company's receptionist, slipped her hand under her desk,
wrapped it around the handgrip of the silencer-fitted SIG
Sauer P226 pistol holstered beneath it, kept her eyes on the
signal light on her telephone switchboard, and waited for
the operatives to clear the six-foot safe zone located inside

the front door. The light remained green. The sophisticated sniffing equipment integrated into the wire mesh WELCOME mat upon which Matt and Kyla stood had not detected the presence of explosive ordnance or deadly chemicals. The light remained green. Had it flashed red, the visitors would have been identified as a security threat. Giselle would have pressed the button on the switchboard. The wire mat would then deliver a fifty-thousand-volt electrical charge through Matt and Kyla's bodies, which would incapacitate them on the spot. Should the TASER-based technology have failed to deliver the intended result, Giselle would have drawn the weapon and shot to wound, not to kill, and the intruders would be detained. The attempted security breach would be dealt with by specialists working in the company whose job it was to extract such information using any means necessary. In this case, the facial recognition software integrated into the camera mounted above the outside entrance door had already scanned Matt and Kyla's faces and acknowledged them as 'C' employees. Their access to the company as 'Classifieds,' or C's, had been approved. She relaxed her grip on the weapon, placed her hands neatly atop the desk, and offered a warm smile. "Nice to meet you, Matt," she said.

Matt smiled. "Same here, Giselle. I'd like you to meet Kyla. We'll be working out of this office for the foreseeable future, together with our colleagues, Roger Morris and Julia Shore. They'll be arriving shortly."

Giselle stood, shook Kyla's hand. "Nice to meet you, Kyla."

Kyla smiled. "And you."

Giselle turned her attention back to Matt. "Your office is

ready for you." She lifted a crystal bowl full of foil wrapped chocolates from her desk, offered them to Matt and Kyla. "Chocolate?" she asked.

Matt took a chocolate from the bowl, unwrapped the sweet treat, popped it into his mouth. "Wow," he said. "They're good."

Giselle smiled. "Yes, they are."

Kyla grabbed a handful from the bowl, winked at Matt. "Product research."

Giselle laughed. "Have as many as you want, but be warned. They'll go straight to your hips. Trust me, I know."

The front door opened. Roger and Julia entered the foyer.

Giselle's eyes shot to the indicator light on the switchboard.

The light remained green.

No threat detected.

Classifieds.

"It's okay," Matt said. "They're with us."

Giselle nodded, took her seat. "Anything you need, press zero to reach me."

"Thanks, Giselle," Matt said. He motioned to Rigor and Jules. "This way."

The four walked through the main office, entered the warehouse, crossed the factory floor. The staff were busy at work. While some tended to the blending machines and production stations, others transferred the sealed and boxed products into master cartons, loaded them on pallets, and prepared them for shipping.

"Quite the operation we've got going here," Rigor said. "When the agency sets up a platform, they do it right."

By platform, Rigor was referring to a CIA cover company.

Matt nodded. "This is more than a platform, Rig," he replied. "Global Confectioners is a legitimate company. The CEO is an American expat and retired military. He lets us use the company as our base of operations."

Rigor jogged over to the assembly line, grabbed two sealed boxes of chocolates from the conveyor belt, ran back, handed one to Julia.

Julia smiled. "Candy, but no flowers. How Rigor of you."

Kyla chuckled. "Sounds like your boyfriend needs a little training in the romance department."

Julia smiled. "Any suggestions?"

Kyla winked at her. "Withholding sex always works for me."

Julia laughed. "I like the way you think."

Rigor opened the box, ate a chocolate. "I don't," he announced.

"Don't worry, Rig," Kyla said. "Julia and I will whip you into shape in no time."

Rigor plopped another chocolate into his mouth. "They're ganging up on me, Gamble. A little backup would be nice."

Matt reached a gray steel door at the back of the warehouse, glanced over his shoulder, smiled. "Sorry, pal. You're on your own."

Rigor grunted. "So much for teamwork." He paused, savored the chocolate. "Mmm. Almond toffee, lightly salted, with a hint of Irish cream and a dash of French vanilla. Perfect texture. This is superb."

"You can tell Cross you approve of our cover," Matt replied. "We have a call with him in ten minutes."

"The old man's not wasting any time."

Matt opened the door. "He never does." He stepped aside, waited. "Ladies, after you."

Kyla and Julia descended the wrought iron spiral staircase, waited for Matt and Rigor at the bottom.

Matt stepped forward, stared into the wall-mounted OCT scanner, waited for the optical coherence tomography device to read the cross-sectioned layers and structures at the back of his eyes. The database confirmed his identity. The handleless steel door clicked open.

Kyla smiled. "Cool. Do we get to play too?"

Matt nodded. "Langley has uploaded everyone's biometrics to the system. Scan in." He opened the door, entered the room. "Welcome to our situation room."

Kyla, Rigor, and Jules scanned in, entered the basement office.

"Damn," Rigor said. "Nice digs."

Jules agreed. "Top-of-the-line tech," she said. "A girl like me could get used to this."

"Every tool a hacker like you would ever need is in this room," Matt said. "Network mapper and web server vulnerability scanners, data packet sniffers, Wi-Fi network routing and firewall security exploitation tools for recon and target system defense testing... and that's just the tech I'm up to speed on. Whatever we don't have, I can get from Cross."

A soft voice spoke through the ceiling-mounted PA system. "Matt?"

"Yes?" Matt replied.

"Sending Langley through to you now."

"Copy that."

The team followed Matt into the boardroom.

A bank of interconnected wall-mounted monitors

displayed the emblem of the Central Intelligence Agency. The static image dissolved as the connection to the encrypted video call was made.

From his office in Langley, Virginia, Task Force Chief Cross stared back at them.

6

Intended Target

MATT GREETED TASK Force Chief Cross as his newly formed team took their seats around the boardroom table in the situation room. "Good morning, sir," he said.

Not one to waste time with pleasantries, Cross addressed the room. "Morris, Shore, Reese... I assume Matt has read you in on NOMAD?"

The team nodded.

Matt replied. "They're up to speed, sir."

"Then I'll get straight to it," Cross replied. "You're being activated. Today."

The wall of monitors came alive as Cross's image dissolved. Each displayed an element of information relevant to the assignment they were about to receive. Faces. Places. Surveillance images.

"The man you're looking at is Hyon Bak. Mr. Bak came to our attention several weeks ago, after defecting to South Korea from North Korea."

Rigor spoke. "How did he manage that?"

"He swam," Cross replied. "Local fisherman plucked him out of the Sea of Japan. He was barely alive. We have an asset inserted in South Korea's National Intelligence Service. He was in the room when Bak was being interviewed. What he had to say came as a shock. This is Armageddon in the making."

The still picture transitioned to a video. Cross explained. "NASA provided this footage through an inter-agency national defense initiative. Think of it as Google Earth on steroids. The building you are looking at is one of ten similar facilities located throughout North Korea, from Sinuiju in the west to Sonbong in the east. We believe they're government labs."

"Labs?" Matt said. "That doesn't make sense. Public healthcare for the North Korean people is practically non-existent. What drugs would they be producing?"

"They're not manufacturing drugs," Cross said. "According to Bak, several weeks prior to his defection, he met with his sister and told her of his plan to escape the country. She told him about a secret government project she is working on codenamed Synoxin-9. The RGB has oversight. There are many Nests located throughout the country. All have been tasked with developing a smart chemical nerve agent for use by the North Korean military."

"Do we know against whom they intend to deploy it?" Kyla asked.

Cross shook his head. "Not yet. But with all the saber

rattling going on lately between the USA, Russia, and North Korea, it's safe to assume we could be the intended target."

"We need to press Bak for information," Rigor said.

"We're working on it," Cross replied. "Our people snatched him off the street in Seoul last week. He's being held at an agency black site. He's refusing to talk until we agree to meet his demands."

"He has demands?" Julia asked.

Cross nodded. "He wants us to extract his sister from North Korea, provide them both with new identities, then relocate them to the United States. Colorado or Wyoming is at the top of his list."

Rigor shook his head. "We're talking about North Korea," he said. "How are we supposed to get in there? In case anybody missed it, we don't exactly look Korean."

"We believe we have a solution for that," Cross said. "Our asset informs us that there's been chatter among the NIS brass. A meeting is taking place next week in Vladivostok, Russia. NASA's space to Earth satellite surveillance mics hit on a keyword its algorithm was instructed to listen for: *han seteu.* Several high-level conversations we've been monitoring mentioned it. It means 'nest' in Korean. It tracks with what Bak told the South Korean government and our people. We believe North Korea might be working with Russia to develop a lethal nerve agent. If that's the case, we need to acquire that intelligence and terminate the project. There's only one way to do that."

"Give Bak what he wants," Matt said.

"Correct," Cross replied. "You'll need to find his sister, extract her, and get her stateside as quickly as possible."

"You want us to crash the party?" Kyla said.

Cross nodded. "Bak's sister is the lead scientist on the

Synoxin-9 project. She'll be in Vladivostok. We know when and where the meeting is taking place. How you get to her is up to you."

"Are you sure Bak can be trusted?" Rigor asked. "He could be setting us up."

"You mean as a double agent?" Cross asked.

Rigor nodded. "Exactly."

Cross shook his head. "He nearly died during his escape. If he were a spy, or a double agent, the North Koreans would have found an easier way to insert him into the country." A woman's face appeared on the screen. "Bak had his sister's photograph taped to his ankle when he was pulled out of the water. This is your extraction target, Dr. Soo Park."

"Pretty lady," Rigor said.

Julia shot him a glance.

Rigor removed a chocolate from the box, unwrapped it, popped it in his mouth, smiled. "What can I say? She is."

Julia rolled her eyes, returned her attention to the screen.

"Dr. Park's meeting takes place in one week," Cross continued. "We need to know everything about NEST and the project they're working on. Your mission is to extract her out of Vladivostok and bring her to the United States. Under no circumstances can she be allowed to return to North Korea. Is that clear?"

Matt nodded. "Crystal, sir."

"Good," Cross said. "I'm texting you a name and number right now. Make use of it if it becomes necessary."

Matt's cellphone chimed. He read the text. "Alexander Kurien. Who's he?"

"He was my protégé and a former CIA counterintelligence officer. Alexander is based in Moscow. He's since left the Agency. Runs a close protection outfit now guarding oligarchs, dignitaries, high rollers... anybody who can afford to pay for his services. He's a good man to know and can get you anything you want should you need it. I'd trust him with my life. We have a safe phrase. Make sure you use it before you say anything else. Tell him Falcon is circling."

"Falcon?"

"My code name when I was in the field."

"Got it."

"All right," Cross said. "I'll leave you to it. Good luck."

Cross's transmission ended. The CIA emblem reappeared on the wall of monitors.

Matt turned to the team. "You heard the man. We have our orders. Go home and pack. We'll meet back here in three hours."

"Where are we going?" Kyla asked.

"Vladivostok," Matt replied.

7

Tug-Of-War

D R. SOO PARK entered her modest home, one of
many similar homes which lined the perfectly
manicured residential street, all of which were
owned by the government and provided to the scientists
working on the NEST project free of charge. Prior to being
assigned to the Hyesan NEST 5 lab, Soo and her family had
lived in similar housing in Kusong, where she was trans-
ported daily to the NEST 3 facility in Manpo. She never
knew which route the bus took to arrive at the NEST, nor
did she want to know. Severe punishment awaited anyone
who tried to remove the cloth hood covering their head
during the journey. She had learned this the hard way. Last
year, one of her colleagues had been caught by the soldier in
charge of their transport for doing so. She was promptly
removed from the bus, taken to the side of the road, and

shot in the head. The passengers overheard the woman's pleas and apologies as she begged him to spare her life and the gunshot that followed. The soldier radioed his supervisor and provided him with a situation report. Ten minutes later, a car arrived. Though the passengers could not see what was happening outside, they heard the conversation taking place between the two men. The woman's lifeless body was placed in the trunk of the supervisor's car. The soldier returned to the bus and warned his passengers to forget everything they had heard or risk meeting a similar fate. The incident was never spoken of again.

Soo removed her coat, hung it on a hook behind the door, and dropped her house keys into a porcelain dish which sat on an ornamental table in the vestibule. She heard her name being called out from the living room, followed by several loud barks. Tam, her son, came running around the corner with his dog, Minho, a Siberian Husky, hot on his heels. The dog's name meant "fast" in Korean, and it suited him well. Minho scooted past Tam and raced down the hall to greet his human mom.

Soo dropped to her knees, took her son and the ecstatic dog in her arms. "Now that's what I call a greeting! How's my boy?"

"Good," Tam replied. "How was work?"

Minho turned, bolted back to the living room, then raced back with his favorite stuffed toy in his mouth. It had been a present from Soo's colleague and friend, Dr. Jin Cho. The dog thrashed the toy back and forth in his mouth, then dropped it at Soo's feet and barked playfully. Soo took the hint, picked up the furry raccoon, tossed the toy down the hall. Minho took off after the toy. Soo walked with Tam down the corridor. "Were you good for Gran?" she asked.

Soo's mother, Tam's grandmother, entered the room. "He's always good for me," she said.

Soo smiled. "That's what I like to hear." Tam plopped down on the couch. She sat beside him. "So, tell me about your day. Did you have fun at school?"

Tam shrugged. "School's boring. Why can't I just come with you to work? I'd learn more. Besides, I want to be a doctor and research scientist just like you when I grow up. You could teach me. Maybe I could have my own lab in a few years."

Soo smiled at her son. "A few years, huh?"

"Sure. Why not?"

"Tam, you're ten. You've got years of study ahead of you before you'll be qualified to get your own lab."

"But I'm smarter than everyone else I know. I could do it."

Tam was right. Two years ago, mandatory government testing had rated his intelligence quotient above 200, which placed his IQ in the range of 'unmeasurable genius,' a level shared by less than five percent of the world's population. For Soo, having a genius for a son came with both pros and cons. Knowing that Tam had the mental capacity to instantly learn anything he put his mind to made her view him with both fascination and fear. He found simple tasks and basic education to be horrendously boring. His was a mind in constant need of stimulation, and the course material he was being force-fed at school made him restless and rambunctious. Next year, he would be transferred to the state university for gifted and exceptional children. Until then, he would remain intellectually unchallenged.

"So, you want your own lab?" Soo asked.

"Yep."

"In what field of study, smarty-pants?"

"I was considering something that would allow me to combine mathematical modeling with applied science," Tam replied matter-of-factly. "Perhaps biomedical engineering with a focus on diagnosis, monitoring, and therapy could be fun. I could create new biomaterials and artificial human tissues. What do you think?"

The look on her son's face gave Soo pause. Tam was completely serious.

"If that's what you want to do, then that's exactly what you should do," she replied.

Tam gave his mother a big smile. "Cool!"

Soo's mother called out from the kitchen where she was busy preparing dinner. "Five minutes, you two. Tam, help me set the table."

"Sure thing, Mom," Soo replied. She leaned over, whispered in her son's ear. "She still talks to me like I'm a little kid."

Tam rolled his eyes. "Tell me about it!"

Soo smiled, stood. "Go help your grandmother. I'll be down in a minute."

"K," Tam replied, then ran to the kitchen with Minho at his side.

SOO CHATTED with her mother and her son while they ate dinner: steamed rice, accompanied by bean paste stew with crab and vegetables, and a side dish of kimchi chock-full of cabbage, radishes, chopped pears, chives, garlic and ginger. When they had finished their meal, Tam helped his mother clear the table and wash the dishes.

"Thanks, Mom," Soo said. "That was delicious."

Soo's mother replied, using the affectionate Korean term for 'sweetheart'. "You're welcome, jagi," she said. She stood, walked to the living room window, parted the shades slightly, and looked outside.

Soo noted the look of concern on her face. "Something wrong, Mom?" she asked.

Tam lay on the floor playing with Minho. The two were engaged in a game of tug-of-war with Minho's toy raccoon. By the look of it, Minho was winning, growling with fake ferocity as he shook his head and tried to wrench the toy free from his master's grasp. Tam released the toy and laughed as the dog tumbled backward. "Ha! Gotcha!" he said. Minho retrieved the toy and crept forward, shaking it once more. Tam grabbed the raccoon by its furry head, pulled hard. The head ripped off the toy.

Soo addressed her mother once again. "Mom, what is it?"

"Probably nothing," her mother replied.

"*What's* probably nothing?"

"The car parked down the street."

"What about it?"

Soo's mother sighed. "This is the third day it's been here. It always arrives just before you get home." She turned and stared at her daughter. "Does that seem unusual to you?"

Soo joined her mother at the window, stared at the car. As if on cue, the vehicle started, then drove slowly past their house.

Tam called out. "Minho, give it to me. Now!"

Soo called out to her son. "Play quietly, you two."

"But Mom," Tam replied.

"No buts, Tam. You heard what I said. Keep it down."

"But Mom... *look*."

Soo turned around. Tam held something in his hand. She walked to him, retrieved the item. "Where did you get this?" she asked.

"It fell out of the raccoon when Minho ripped its head off. What is it?"

Soo felt the blood rush out of her face. She stared at her mother and her son, brought a finger to her lips to silence them, then walked to the kitchen counter, removed the lid from the cookie jar, dropped the device into the container, resealed the vacuum lid, tore a sheet of paper from the notepad beside the phone, scribbled a note, handed the paper to her mother.

Her mother looked at her daughter, eyes wide with concern.

Soo's note read, THE RGB IS LISTENING.

8

A Little Advice

HREE HOURS LATER, Matt and his team rendezvoused back at Global Confectioners as planned, then made the short drive to Grantley Adams International Airport. At the ground transportation security gate, Matt presented the electronic credentials Cross had emailed him to the guard. Similar credentials had been provided for each team member. Rigor, Kyla, and Julia presented their phones to the guard. Each was scanned and verified.

"Just the four of you today?" the guard asked.

Matt smiled. The false credentials identified them as flight attendants with Delta Air Lines. "As far as I know," Matt said. "Can you check the computer and confirm whether the captain and his SFC have arrived yet?"

The guard punched the keys on his computer keyboard,

nodded. "Captain Arden is on the aircraft now. Senior First Officer Galloway arrived five minutes ahead of you." The security guard shook his head. "Man, it must be nice to jet around the world on the airline's dime."

Matt smiled. "The job has its perks."

The guard pressed a button on his console. Matt waited for the gate to roll aside, then waved to the guard as he drove through.

Rigor spoke as Matt drove to the restricted hangar Cross informed him was reserved for the agency's exclusive use. "We have our own plane?"

Matt pointed to the pushback truck pulling the massive Delta Air Lines Airbus A350 out of its hangar to its standby position on the tarmac. "We do."

Rigor whistled. "I'll be damned."

"Cross emailed me while I was waiting for you to arrive and gave me the heads-up about the hangar. He told me he'd be lending us a few toys."

Kyla spoke. "When the TFC said you'd have access to everything you'd need, he wasn't kidding."

"Apparently not," Julia said.

"Seeing that I'm a licensed pilot," Rigor said, "you think the captain would let me take over the stick for a few hundred miles?"

Matt smiled. "Are you asking me if he'd let a guy whose flight experience is limited to single-engine aircraft take over the controls of a three-hundred-and-twenty-million-dollar CIA air asset?"

Rigor grinned. "I am."

Matt shook his head. "Not on your life, pal."

With the Airbus now clear of the massive hangar, Matt drove his silver Range Rover inside and parked. "Follow me," he said. "Cross said we need to familiarize ourselves with the facility."

Kyla stepped out of the vehicle, looked around. "What's there to familiarize ourselves with?" she asked. "It's a big, empty box. The plane goes in, the plane goes out. Seems pretty straightforward to me."

"I'm guessing there's more to this place than meets the eye," Matt replied. He walked to an electrical breaker panel mounted on the wall beside the hangar's massive rollback door, followed the instructions Task Force Chief Cross had provided to him. He opened the panel cover, ran his finger down the breakers, found the one that was unlabeled, then flipped it three times. Several feet away, a mechanical assembly whirred. The team watched as a six-foot-wide airline mechanic's tool chest slid aside, its weight supported by the steel platform upon which it stood. Lights suddenly came on, illuminating a staircase leading to a room below the hangar floor.

"First the secret room at Global Confectioners and now this," Rigor said. "Sweet."

The team followed Matt down the stairs into the massive supply room. Together, they explored the facility. Kyla opened the floor-to-ceiling cabinets, checked out their contents, shook her head. "There's enough ordnance in this room to level the airport."

Rigor called out from across the room. "Hey, check this out. HALO jumpsuits!"

"HALO?" Julia asked.

Rigor nodded. "The ultimate in extreme parachuting. HALO is an acronym. It stands for High Altitude Low Opening. HALO parachutists jump from insanely high altitudes, then deploy their chute at the very last minute. It's one hell of a rush, but not if you're the type to panic and freeze up. Then you'll have a problem."

"What kind of problem?" Kyla asked.

"You'll be introduced to the ground in a hurry. Splatsville. Pancake city."

"Can't say I like the sound of that," Julia stated.

"Don't worry," Matt said. "Each of you will become familiar with HALO jumps and how to do them safely."

"Why is that?" Kyla asked.

"Because that's how we're getting into Russia."

"We're HALO jumping out of the Airbus?" Rigor asked.

Matt nodded. "That's right."

"You're talking about jumping from an altitude of forty-three thousand feet."

"Yes, I am."

Rigor nodded and smiled. "This is gonna be sooo cool!"

"About the jump," Matt continued. "There is one minor detail I haven't mentioned."

"What's that?" Kyla asked.

"We'll be jumping at night. In the dark. Gauges only."

Julia raised her hand.

"Yes?" Matt said.

"Quick question."

"Shoot."

"Is it too late to back out of this gig?"

Matt smiled. "I'm afraid so."

Rigor nudged Julia's shoulder. "Can I offer a little advice?"

Julia nodded. "Sure."

"Don't eat much on the plane. The jump won't go well if you throw up in your oxygen mask on the way down. Makes it harder to read your gauges." He slapped his hands together for emphasis. *Splat*.

Julia smiled, batted her eyelashes. "Good talk," she replied. "Can I offer *you* a little advice?"

Rigor smiled. "Sure, hon."

"Shut up."

9

Under Suspicion

"TAM, GO TO your room," Soo said.

Tam threw his hands up in objection. "What did I do?"

"Nothing, son."

"Then why are you sending me to my..."

Soo raised her voice. "Now, Tam."

Tam stormed off. "Man, this sucks." Minho followed at his heels, his tail swishing back and forth. Tam looked down at the dog. "Why are you so happy? You broke the toy, not me!"

The dog chuffed, gave its master a puzzled look, then followed him into his room.

Soo and her mother heard Tam's bedroom door slam shut.

Soo's mother spoke. "You shouldn't have spoken to him like that. It's not his fault."

"You think I don't know that?" Soo replied, her tone anxious.

"Can they hear us now?" her mother asked.

Soo shrugged, shook her head. "Yes... no... maybe. I don't know how powerful that device is."

"It was a gift from your friend, wasn't it?"

Soo nodded.

Soo's mother whispered. "You think she's working for the RGB?"

"We all work for the RGB, Mother," Soo replied.

"You know what I mean. Not as a scientist, but as a spy."

"Why would anyone want to spy on me? I'm a nobody."

"You're hardly a nobody, Soo," her mother said. "You're a lead scientist working for the Supreme Leader in a facility to which you're driven in secret every day. It stands to reason they might want to keep tabs on you."

"There are cameras in the lab that watch me every second of the day, Mother. What else would they want to know? I have a family life that is as normal as anyone else's."

"They don't know that."

"What are you saying?"

"That you're also human. Wives talk to husbands, husbands talk to wives. Some things are better left unsaid."

"I never spoke to Seok about my work. He knew I wasn't permitted to, so he never asked."

"What about Tam?"

"Tam?"

"You know how much he idolizes you. He's a ten-year-old boy who's read every scientific textbook he's been able to get his hands on and has committed the information to memory. Smart doesn't even come close to describing his intellectual ability. Don't fool yourself. If he hasn't yet figured out exactly what it is you're working on, he will soon."

"Are you saying Tam might be who the RGB is spying on and not me?"

"The listening device was hidden in Minho's toy, wasn't it?"

Soo nodded. "Yes."

"And who is Minho always playing with?"

"Tam."

"That's right. Those two are connected at the hip. Except for school, Tam goes nowhere without Minho, and Minho goes nowhere without his raccoon. He loves that toy. Personally, I don't know why. It's damn ugly."

Soo paused.

"What are you thinking?" her mother asked.

"Perhaps it's not even that."

"Then what?"

"Not what, but who. Hyon."

"Your brother?"

Soo nodded.

"There's nothing more you could tell the RGB about Hyon than you already have when they interviewed you, as did I. Neither of us knows why he defected."

"The Reconnaissance General Bureau doesn't have a reputation for taking people at their word," Soo affirmed. "Maybe they think I'm still in contact with him."

"That would be impossible."

"We know that, but the RGB doesn't."

"If you ask me, your friend from work is behind this. God only knows what she's trying to do to you... to us."

"Jin? But why?"

Soo's mother shrugged. "Professional jealousy perhaps? Always being seen as your number two?"

"That's ridiculous. Jin doesn't feel that way. No single scientist is given credit for the discoveries we make. It's a team effort."

"If it's such a team effort, why were you named *lead* scientist? Isn't that what you told me when you received your promotion? It's also why the RGB moved us into this unit, one that is so much larger and nicer than the others."

"But I've done nothing wrong. I haven't given the RGB a single reason to suspect me of anything."

"*You* haven't said or done anything. But maybe Jin has."

"I don't understand."

"Maybe she wants what she can't have."

"Meaning?"

"Recognition. A bigger house. To be seen by others as being more important than you. To bring you down."

"That's crazy. We're leaving together for Russia in a few days."

Soo's mother's eyes widened. "Russia? When were you planning on telling me this?"

"After dinner. You went to the window and distracted me. We've been asked to present our discovery in Vladivostok."

"You're presenting your work to the Russians?"

Soo nodded.

"And that doesn't strike you as strange?"

"It's not my place to question why, Mother. This meeting is incredibly important. I'm sure there are political reasons for it as well, although I don't know what they are, nor do I want to know." Soo turned and walked away. "I've already told you more than I should have."

Soo's mother responded thoughtfully. "Perhaps the best thing to do in this situation is give the RGB and Jin something they won't expect."

Soo shook her head. "I don't follow."

"Tam has been publicly recognized as the smartest child in North Korea. The Supreme Leader will expect great things from him in the future."

"What are you getting at?"

"Give the Supreme Leader another reason to show the Russians that the people of North Korea are more intellectually advanced than they are. Convince your supervisors at the RGB to reach out to him and get his approval to allow Tam to present *something* at this meeting in Vladivostok. It doesn't matter what he presents, just as long as he shows off his incredible mind and leaves them speechless."

"Don't be ridiculous, Mother. The Supreme Leader would never allow a ten-year-old boy to speak at a conference of this importance. The scientists who will be attending have been handpicked. They are the best of the best."

"Have you ever known our Supreme Leader to miss an opportunity to show off North Korea's superiority to the world?"

"No."

"Then why not let him do the same with the State's most gifted child? Both you and Tam would be seen by everyone as being completely transparent, with nothing to hide. If Jin has been working with the RGB in an effort to discredit you, you'll have shut her down. Who knows? Perhaps you'll turn the tables, and she'll become the one under suspicion. You'll fall right off the RGB's radar. Surely you can see the benefit of what I'm proposing."

Soo nodded. "I can."

"Then find a way for Tam to attend that presentation with you."

Night had fallen. Beyond the window, the beam of a car's headlights passed by the window.

"Turn off the lights," Soo's mother said. "Do it quickly!"

Soo flipped off the living room and kitchen lights, and plunged the main floor into darkness.

Mother and daughter crept to the living room window, parted the curtains, looked out.

"It's the same car we saw before," Soo said.

Soo's mother nodded. "It's back."

10

Silverware and Bottle Service

FOLLOWING MATT'S INSTRUCTIONS, the team gathered the gear they would require for their mission and boarded the A350 jetliner.

"Well," Kyla said as she cleared the air stairs and stepped inside the massive plane. "This isn't exactly what I was expecting."

From the tarmac, the aircraft markings were the same as any other commercial jetliner in Delta's fleet, but the inside of the plane was completely different in its layout and design. The forward compartment, which on any of Delta's other A350s would have offered luxurious seating and immaculate appointments for its first and executive class passengers was gone. So, too, were its secondary passenger seating areas. The entire plane was essentially empty. Floor-to-ceiling cargo nets ran down both sides of the aircraft.

Metal seats, which were affixed to the walls, were folded up in their closed positions. Across from the row of seats, long nets swayed as a warm Caribbean breeze passed through the open cabin door.

"How quaint," Julia said as she entered the Airbus behind Kyla. She dropped a heavy canvas bag, which contained an assortment of weapons and armaments, on the floor. She turned to Kyla. "You ever watch those corny home renovation shows on TV?"

Kyla nodded. "Yeah."

"You know how they show you what the place looked like *before* it got its makeover?"

"Uh-huh."

"This is the airline equivalent of that."

Kyla laughed. "Where's Martha when you need her?"

Rigor followed Matt into the plane. He inhaled deeply, exhaled. "Ahh," he said. "Don't you just love the noxious smell of aviation fuel first thing in the morning?"

Matt shook his head. "Not particularly."

Rigor smiled, took in another deep breath, held it, let it out emphatically. "Just wakes up the senses, doesn't it? Makes you feel alive."

"Know what would wake up my senses and make me feel alive?" Julia said. "A hot cup of coffee. The stronger, the better."

Matt pointed. "There's a coffee station right behind you, Jules. Food too. It's heat-and-eat military rations, but it tastes good."

"This is the Agency," Rigor said. He turned to his girl-friend and smiled. "What were you expecting? Silverware and bottle service?"

"No, but I will when we get back," Julia replied. "And you better deliver, buster."

Rigor laughed. "Yes, ma'am."

"Stow your gear and grab a seat," Matt said. "It's going to be a long flight. We'll go over the plan when we're in the air. Rig, you'll take us through a HALO jump orientation and familiarize us with the gear and how to use it."

"You've got it, boss," Rigor replied.

"Quick overview of the plane," Matt said. "Two washrooms, one in the front, one in the back." He spread open one of the many horizontal nets which hung from the ceiling. "Hammocks. They might take a little getting used to. Once you do, you'll sleep like a baby."

"Better assign Rigor to one near the back of the plane," Julia quipped. "The man snores like a freight train."

"No problem," Matt said. "If he gets too loud, I'll toss him out somewhere over the Atlantic."

Julia glanced at Matt, batted her eyes, smiled. "Aww... you'd do that for me? How sweet."

Matt nodded. "It would be my pleasure."

Walking toward the lavatory at the back of the aircraft, Rigor looked over his shoulder, called out. "Heard that."

"Just kidding, sweetheart," Julia replied, then mouthed a word to Matt: *Not.*

Matt picked up the bags the team had brought aboard and laid them beside one another in the middle of the aircraft. "Give me a minute to speak to the captain," he said. "You two settle in."

Julia and Kyla nodded. "Buy you a coffee?" Julia asked.

Kyla smiled. "You bet."

Matt knocked on the flight deck door. A buzzer sounded;

the door unlocked. Matt stepped inside and closed the door behind him. "How are we looking?" he asked.

Captain Arden and Senior First Officer Galloway nodded. "Pre-flight's almost complete," Arden replied. "Say," he said. "Are those HALO jumpsuits you brought on board?"

Matt nodded. "Yes."

"There's a dedicated compartment at the back of the aircraft you'll need to use for HALO drops," Arden said. "When you're ready, press the green button on the wall. As soon as the compartment pressurizes, you'll be good to go. What type of chutes are you using?"

"High-performance, with tapered tactical canopies."

"Should offer a tight landing. Where's the drop zone?"

"The Livandyskaya mountain region, outside Vladivostok."

Arden nodded. "The Livandyskayas skirt the Russian and North Korean borders. Your team will have to jump before we inform Vladivostok that we're on final approach."

"No problem. How long until we're off the ground?"

Arden glanced at his Senior First Officer for the answer. "Ground and systems checks are complete," Galloway replied. "We'll be off the tarmac in ten minutes. Flight time is fourteen hours, so you'll have plenty of time to rest up. Tell your people to buckle in."

"Copy that," Matt replied. "Safe flight."

Arden nodded. "Good luck with your mission."

Matt left the flight deck, closed the door behind him. He called out as Rigor returned from the lavatory. "Everybody take a seat and tuck in. Captain's orders."

Kyla sat beside Matt, Julia beside Rigor.

Matt felt Kyla's hand slip into his.

As the Airbus taxied down the runway and lifted off, she squeezed it tightly.

11

Nothing Is Impossible

THE RGB OPERATIVES sat in their car, observed the house, watched as the lights suddenly went out and the house went dark. A single light illuminated an upstairs room.

Curious, the senior operative checked his watch. The scientist they had been assigned to monitor had arrived home from work an hour ago, far too early to be retiring for the night. He spoke to his subordinate. "That's odd."

The younger man looked at his boss. "What is?"

"The lights in the living room just went out."

"So?"

"That doesn't strike you as strange?"

"Maybe they're watching television."

"In the dark?"

"That's how I watch TV, don't you?"

"Never. I always have a light on. Those sudden scene transitions from dark screen to bright light kill my eyes. Having a light on helps."

The young man teased his superior. "That's because you're not as young and spry as you used to be. You know what they say."

"What's that?"

"Declining eyesight is the first sign of getting older."

"Not true. My knees beat my eyes to it."

"Maybe you should give some thought to hanging it up."

The senior operative shook his head. "Never gonna happen."

"How long have you been with the RGB?" the young man asked.

"Twenty years."

"Why so long?"

"Because I like what I do," his superior replied. "I keep the country safe. To me, there is no higher calling. I consider it an honor and a privilege to do this job. You should too."

The young man sighed. "I suppose."

"That didn't sound very convincing."

"Sorry." The rookie had been assigned to work with the senior operative, now his field training officer. "I'm second generation RGB," he continued. "My father retired last year. The commendation letter he received on his last day of service from our Supreme Leader is on display in my parents' living room."

"He's obviously very proud of it, and justifiably so."

The young man nodded. "Except I didn't have a choice. He decided my future for me. All he'd ever talk about to his friends was how proud he'd be when the time finally came for me to join the RGB and follow in his footsteps."

"Aren't you?"

The junior operative shrugged. "There are worse jobs."

"You're half my age and you're already in the intelligence unit. Do you have any idea how much of an accomplishment that is? It takes most rookies years to get to that position. You got in right out of the gate."

"That didn't happen through my efforts alone. Sure, I aced my courses. But my father was a high-ranking and respected member of the RGB. He'd spent most of his career in intelligence. I'm sure a few strings got pulled to make that happen."

"Regardless, you wouldn't be sitting next to me if Command didn't think you have what it takes to succeed in the role."

The young man smiled. "Thanks."

"Which begs the question."

"What's that?"

"What would you have done with your life if the RGB had refused to let you join the Bureau?"

The man nodded at the house they were watching. "I'd be doing what Dr. Park is doing. I'd be a research scientist."

The older man joked with his protégé. "So, you're saying you're smarter than you look?"

The younger man laughed. "You're the one evaluating my performance. I'll let you decide that for yourself."

"Fair enough." The senior operative paused, picked up the listening device's handheld monitor, tapped its case several times. "That's strange."

"What is?"

"Listen."

The young man paused. "I don't hear anything."

"Exactly. The bug has stopped working."

The young man held out his hand. "May I see it?"

His training officer handed him the equipment. "You're an electronics genius, too?"

"No, but I have a way with gadgets. I can fix just about anything."

"Fine. Just don't break it. That thing costs more than I make in a year."

The young man fiddled with the device's buttons, played with its switches and dials. Several seconds later, the bug that had been planted inside the dog's toy in the Park family home came back online.

"Well, I'll be," the senior operative said. "You *are* smarter than you look."

The young man chuckled. "Must have been a glitch."

"Glitch or not, we're back in business. Nice going."

The lights on the main floor of the house came back on.

"What do you suppose that was about?"

"Was *what* about?" the young man asked.

"The sudden blackout. Strikes me as odd that the bug would go down for the same amount of time as the lights were out."

The young man shrugged. "It's probably just a coincidence. Why the round-the-clock surveillance on Dr. Park anyway? Did she do something wrong?"

"No, but her brother did."

"Meaning?"

"We thought he'd drowned. Turns out he hadn't. We have it on good authority he made it to South Korea."

"He defected?"

The older operative nodded. "Dr. Park has been red carded because of her brother's actions. The RGB wants to know if she's still in contact with him."

"But that would be impossible, wouldn't it?"

"Believe me, son, if you choose to continue with your career in the RGB, you'll need to learn a very important lesson right now."

"And that is?"

"In the world of intelligence, nothing is impossible."

12

A Long Flight

THE FLIGHT CREW turned off the fasten seatbelt sign after the plane had leveled off. Matt unbuckled his belt, left his chair, opened one of the bags he had brought aboard the aircraft. He inspected the various defensive weapons and armaments he had gathered from the secret room beneath the agency's private hangar.

"Flight time to Vladivostok is fourteen hours," Matt called out. "Time to go over the plan. After that, hit the racks and get some sleep. I'll start. When I'm finished, Rigor will familiarize us with the HALO equipment we'll be using and take us through the jump protocol."

Rigor nodded. "Got it."

"Good," Matt said. "This mission will be unlike anything any of us has done before. Our drop location will put us in close contact with Russian state security forces, which means we need to get creative in terms of how we arm and defend ourselves should it come down to it. I'd like nothing more than for this mission to go off without a hitch, but you know what they say about best laid plans."

"There's no such thing," Kyla said.

Matt nodded. "Exactly." He removed several thin plastic cylinders from the bag, handed one to each member of the team. "Unscrew the cylinder and remove the pen."

The team followed Matt's instructions. "What you're holding is a new toy from the agency. It's a dual-purpose defensive device: an auto injector pen and IED. It's made entirely of plastic. Note the caps on both ends. One is orange, the other purple. There is a revolving sleeve positioned above each cap. First, the orange end. Rotating its sleeve will reload the pen. It contains a small needle and a vial of general anesthetic which, when plunged into the neck, arm, chest, or leg of an adversary, will deliver a non-lethal dose of liquid halothane directly into their bloodstream. The effect will be immediate. They'll fall asleep instantly and wake up hours later. You can reuse it twenty times before the vial is empty."

"And the purple end?" Jules asked.

"That's the end that goes bang. Remember these 3T's: *twist, toss, take cover*. Discard the purple cap, twist its sleeve once, then toss it and take cover. It contains RX-27, which is a blast gel. It looks like purple jelly, is odorless, and was chemically engineered so that it can't be identified by bomb sniffing equipment or K-9s trained in plastic explosives detection."

"What's its detonation capability?" Kyla asked.

"It'll blow a six-foot hole in a concrete wall, no problem."

Kyla smiled. "Sweet."

"We won't be able to carry firearms into the convention room," Matt continued. "There'll likely be metal detectors at the hall entrance door, so we'll have to improvise." He handed both Kyla and Jules a small jewelry box. The women opened the boxes, removed two large, half-moon-shaped earrings.

"They're beautiful," Jules said. "I take it that they serve a purpose other than being a pretty fashion accessory?"

"They do," Matt said. He took one earring from Kyla, pressed on the front and back of the half-moon. The earring opened like a pocketknife into two connected halves. "Open it like this, discard the earlobe hook, and it becomes a perfectly balanced throwing blade."

"Talk about a killer accessory," Rigor said.

Jules shook her head. "That was bad... really bad!"

Rigor smiled. "I could have said the idea was out of this world... you know... moon, out of this world?"

Matt stared at Rig. "Mind if I continue?"

Rigor nodded. "Sorry, boss. My bad."

Matt held up a small, round container. "This might look like a standard pocket pill carrier, but it's not. The spool inside holds one hundred feet of RX-27 translucent microfilament receiver enabled Detcord. Pull out the length you need. A cutter is built into the lid. Attach it to any surface. Clicking the container lid three times will activate the RF transmitter. Send the signal and that section of Detcord will go boom. I don't recommend being anywhere near it when it does."

"Please tell me you have a fancy watch in there that has all kinds of cool uses," Rigor said.

"Sorry," Matt replied. "Not this time."

Rigor shook his head. "Damn."

"Last but not least, two ceramic knives for close-quarters combat. A word of advice: the fewer bodies we leave behind, the better. We need to get in, acquire the target, and get out as fast as possible. Questions?"

No response.

"That's it," Matt said. "There are pockets inside your HALO suit to stow this stuff. Rig, take us through the jump."

"Happy to," Rigor said. He jogged to the front of the plane, grabbed a large duffle bag, dragged it back to the team, unzipped it. "Alright boys and girls, welcome to HALO Jumping 101." He removed the high altitude, low opening parachute jumping equipment from the bag, explained the use of each element as he suited up. "First, the jump suit itself. At forty-three thousand feet, which is the height from which we'll be jumping, the air is damn cold. The suit is made from Cordura nylon and features forward-facing thermal insulation located in the chest, arms, legs, and collar which will protect you against extreme cold, wind, rain, and even snow during the drop. Notice the Velcro closures at the wrists and ankles. They serve a dual purpose. First, they keep the suit in place during freefall. Second, they keep the heat in and your body warm. Inside you'll find pockets for maps, chem-lights, a radio pouch. That's it for the suit itself. Next, gloves and boots. Gloves go on the hands; boots go on the feet. Don't mix that up. If you do, you'll look stupid when you jump out of the aircraft. Next, the helmet and goggles. Goggles go over your eyes, head goes inside the helmet. Make sure to fasten the chinstrap." He held up a large watch-like instrument. "This is called an altimeter. Fasten it around your wrist like a watch. It indicates how high up you are and measures changes in altitude all the way to the ground. Keep an eye on it. This is a low-opening jump, which means we'll be waiting until the last possible second to open our chutes. Speaking of which, this is your harness, also called a container. Anybody care to guess why it's called that? Because it *contains* both the main canopy and your reserve chute. It's made of ripstop nylon, so there's no chance that it will tear. The ripcord is right here. Pull it when I tell you to and not before. This is your oxygen supply. The air up there is too thin to breathe. Place the mask over your nose and mouth, secure its snaps to your helmet, turn on your oxygen, and breathe normally. Don't worry, you've got plenty of air for the jump. When you exit the aircraft, bend your knees. Your feet will lift up behind you. That's normal, so don't try to fight it. Angle your arms out at your sides like you're signaling left and right hand turns. We'll suit up ten minutes before jump time and double check our gear. We'll be on comms throughout the drop, so listen for me to give the word when to deploy your chute. Do that and you'll be perfectly fine. Don't do that and this jump will literally be the last thing you'll remember. Everyone clear on that?"

Matt, Kyla, and Jules nodded.

"Good," Rigor said. He turned to Matt. "Class dismissed."

"Thanks, Rig," Matt said. "We've got a long flight ahead of us. Everyone grab a hammock and bed down. The crew will notify us when we're approaching Russian airspace."

Quiet fell over the team as they took to their hammocks and settled in for the remainder of the flight to Vladivostok.

Thirteen hours until mission execution.

13

All But Impossible

SOO REMOVED THE listening device from the cookie jar, placed it on the counter, scribbled another note, handed it to her mother: TAKE MINHO FOR A WALK.

Her mother nodded and called out. "Tam, honey. Minho needs to go for a walk. So do I."

Tam called down from his upstairs bedroom. "But Gran, I'm reading!"

"You can finish reading when we get back."

"Do I have to?" Tam objected.

Soo played bad cop for her mother. "If Minho doesn't go out right now, you know what he'll do. Do you want to be the one cleaning up after him?"

Tam's reply carried with it a tone of defeat. "No."

"Then you have your answer. Downstairs, young man."

Tam closed his book, left his room, sulked down the stairs, plopped his butt down on the bottom step, slipped into his running shoes, grabbed his jacket, pulled on his baseball cap, and called out. "Minho! Walkies!"

The Husky let out a excited bark, then bounded out of the living room. He ran to his master and pawed at Tam's running shoes as Tam removed his leash from the hook beside the door.

"Okay, okay," Tam said. "Cool your jets!" He fastened the dog's leash to its collar, opened the door. "Ready, Gran," he announced.

"Be right there," came the reply.

Soo wrote another note, presented it to her mother: GIVE ME TWENTY MINUTES.

Her mother nodded in agreement, noted the worried look on her daughter's face, hugged her, kissed her cheek. She announced her departure for the benefit of whoever was listening. "We're just going around the block. Back in twenty minutes."

"Sounds good," Soo replied.

Her mother tore off a sheet of paper from the notepad, jotted down a message, handed it to her daughter: FLUSH THESE NOTES NOW.

Soo nodded and walked with her mother to the door. Minho whined and pawed at the floor, eager to go for his walk.

Tam spoke sternly to the dog. "Wait until I get the door open, will ya? Geez!"

Minho nosed his way through the crack in the open door, pulled his master outside behind him. Together, they bounded down the steps and headed out for their walk.

"I'd better catch up with them before they're out of sight," Soo's mother said.

Soo laughed. "I think you're right."

"Back soon, honey. Love you."

"Love you too, mom."

Soo watched her mother follow after her son and their dog.

The vehicle they had observed earlier was still parked down the street. Although its windows were tinted, the light from the sodium vapor streetlamp under which the car sat cast a jaundiced glow over the windshield and revealed the presence of two individuals. Soo stole a glance at the license plate in the pale light.

It showed two groups of white numbers, separated by a hyphen, on a black background.

The car was military, its occupants most likely agents with the Reconnaissance General Bureau.

Soo waved goodbye to her mother, closed the door, then searched her house for additional devices.

Twenty minutes later, when her mother, son, and dog had returned home, she whispered her findings into her mother's ear: "Nothing."

Satisfied with the report, her mother nodded. It made sense. She was home alone during the day while her daughter was at work and her grandson attended school. The Park home was not large, and she knew every sound it made. Had she been anywhere in the house when someone had tried to enter it without permission, she would have heard it. If she had been in the bathroom, Minho would have assumed his usual position outside the door, waiting until she rejoined him. There had been no visits to the home for as long as she could remember. Had someone tried to enter the home during the night while they were sleeping, Minho would have heard them, barked, awoken the household, and investigated the source of the intrusion.

"Perhaps you should submit that request for Tam to join you in Russia tonight, before it's too late," Soo's mother suggested.

Soo nodded. "That's a good idea."

"We'll watch television when you're finished."

"Sounds good."

"Something funny. A comedy."

"I could use a little cheering up."

"Yes, you could."

Soo headed upstairs to her office to email the request to her superiors. She sat at her desk, opened her computer, and played absently with the dolphin charm attached to her necklace. She thought about her brother and how he had told her of his plan to escape North Korea by swimming south through the Sea of Japan. It had been an incredible accomplishment.

In three days, she too would accomplish something which, until now, had seemed all but impossible. She would have the opportunity to see how others outside of her country lived.

Soo focused her thoughts and started to type.

14

Move Like Water

MATT LAY IN his hammock, listening to the drone of the A350s engines as the aircraft journeyed toward Russia. Kyla lay in the adjoining hammock. She whispered. "You awake?"

Matt swung his feet over the side of the suspended bed and sat up. "Yeah."

Kyla rolled onto her stomach, looked at him. "Get any sleep?"

Matt shook his head. "Not a wink."

"Thinking about the mission?"

Matt nodded.

Kyla assured him. "We're going to be fine, Matt."

"I hope so."

"You think we won't?"

Matt shrugged. "Call it pre-game jitters."

Kyla smiled. "A little anticipation is a good thing. It means you're alert and paying attention."

"I know."

"What else is bothering you?"

Matt sighed. "I'm concerned about Rigor."

"Concerned how?"

"He's the one member of the team I don't really know at all."

"You selected him for the team, didn't you?"

"Yeah."

"Then why are you having second thoughts about him now?"

"Because I know how you and Jules perform in the field under pressure. I've seen it. I have confidence in both of you to get the job done. I brought Rigor on board because of his reputation in the agency, but I've never worked with him directly before. Plus, he's beginning to strike me as a bit of a renegade. I hope that doesn't become a problem."

"The command order has been established, Matt," Kyla assured him. "He knows you're in charge of this team. Cross made that clear in our videoconference."

"Rigor's a hotshot and he knows it," Matt replied. "Plus, he's got the skills to back it up."

Kyla nodded. "True. The agency didn't codename him Coroner for nothing."

"I'm not questioning the guy's credentials as a top tier assassin," Matt replied. "What concerns me is how much of a team player he is... or isn't."

"Are you worried that he'll disobey a command?"

Matt's demeanor was stoic, focused. "Lives are on the line here, Kyla. Yours, mine, Jules... not to mention our targets. This operation has to run smoothly. Nothing can go wrong. If it does, we could end up spending the rest of our lives in a Russian gulag. Personally, I'm not fond of labor detention camps, be they in Russia or any other part of the world."

Kyla smiled. "You mean the idea of breaking up rocks with a sledgehammer and eating watery porridge, cold soup, mashed potatoes, and rancid fish for breakfast, lunch, and dinner seven days a week doesn't appeal to you?"

Matt shook his head. "I'm more of a burger and fries kind of guy."

Kyla reached out, took his hand in hers. "You've made good choices, Matt. Your team is solid. We've got this. We'll come together and get the job done, you'll see. Besides, we all know this particular mission is impossible to prep for. Planning is one thing, execution is another. We've come together as one. Now, we move like water and burn like fire. Best-case scenario, we do so without the bad guys even knowing what hit them. In and out, wham bam, thank you ma'am. Everyone is highly trained. And you might not know it, but you're already building a team. I can see it in their eyes. They respect you. And so they should. Cross put you in charge of NOMAD for a reason. He didn't offer that role to anyone else. If he didn't have total confidence in you to put together the right group of people who could pull this off, I can guarantee you that NOMAD would still be a black ops project in concept only, but it isn't. We've been activated, and we're going to do everything within our ability to achieve the objectives Cross has set for us, for this mission, and beyond. And we'll do it with *you* leading us."

Matt smiled. "Maybe Cross should have put you in charge of NOMAD. There's no way I could ever deliver a speech like that."

Kyla grinned. "It was pretty good, wasn't it?"

"Tony Robbins would be proud."

"Hey, don't mess with Tony. He rocks."

Matt laughed. "Yes, he does."

Kyla slipped out of her hammock. "Scoot over," she said. She sat next to Matt. "We're going to do great, Matt. I know it."

Matt nodded. "Yeah, we will."

"Besides," Kyla continued. "If NOMAD doesn't work out, I have a backup plan."

"You do?"

"Yep."

"What's that?"

"I'm going to get Tony's number, give him a ring, and ask him to set me up on the motivational speaking circuit."

"Is that so?"

"Yeppers."

"Just how do you plan to get his number? I'm pretty sure he's a hard guy to get a hold of, what with him running a gazillion businesses and all."

Kyla nudged his shoulder. "I'm CIA, remember? I know people who know people. I can have his cell phone cracked in seconds. Piece of cake."

"Have you ever been told you have a devious mind?"

Kyla smiled. "I do, don't I?"

"Yes, you do."

"Is that one of the reasons why you love me?"

"One, yes."

"What are the others?"

Matt sighed, considered his answer. "Hmm, let me see. Great cook... excellent housekeeper... you let me leave the toilet seat up. By the way, you get bonus points for that last one."

Kyla crossed her arms. "*Really?*"

Matt smiled. "Killer bod... great in bed...easy on the eye..."

"Much better."

Matt laughed. He turned to Kyla, looked into her eyes. "I love you because you are the best thing that's ever happened to me. You're all I could ever ask for and then some."

Kyla smiled. "Now, that's more like it." She looked down at Matt's hammock. "Think there's enough room in there for two?"

Matt grinned. "I think we can make it work."

Kyla winked. "I was hoping you'd say that."

15

Lights Out

THE RGB OPERATIVES watched as Dr. Park's son, his grandmother, and their family dog returned home. As Tam opened the door for his grandmother, Minho pushed his way past them and bounded inside.

Through the listening device's monitor, the senior operative paid close attention to the conversation that followed. How was the walk? Good. Did Minho do his business? Four times. The boy talked about reaching a new high score on his video game, then asked his mother if she would take him to the library on the weekend. The next hour consisted of unremarkable discussions related to trivial family matters. No telephone calls or late-night visitors were received. So far, the evening's surveillance had proved uneventful, as had their previous days spent monitoring the house.

"This seems like a waste of time," the junior operative said.

His field training officer nodded. "I'm beginning to believe that, too."

"Did we have anything on Dr. Park before we began monitoring her?"

The senior operative shook his head. "Nothing but suspicion."

"That she was in contact with her brother?"

"Correct."

"We've been watching the home for a week. If they had been in communication with each other, wouldn't we have learned about it by now?"

The senior operative paused. "That's a difficult question to answer."

"Why?"

"We have only one bug in the house. The one in the dog's toy."

"We should have placed more."

"Yes."

"What about her devices? Are they being monitored?"

The senior operative nodded. "Cell phone, laptop, home phone... the works."

"For how long?"

"Since the brother disappeared."

"And?"

"Nothing."

The junior operative let out a heavy sigh. "I don't know. My gut is telling me there's nothing here."

"And you're basing this observation on what? Your *many years* of field experience?"

"No, I'm basing it on the fact that we've made absolutely

no progress with this stakeout since it began. Maybe Dr. Park has nothing to hide."

The senior operative nodded. "You could be right." He checked his watch. "We'll give it fifteen more minutes."

"Sounds good."

Upstairs in the Park household, they watched a light go out.

Soo finished writing the email asking for permission for Tam to join her at the conference, sent it to her boss, shut down her computer, then turned off her desk lamp and went downstairs to join her mother.

Tam sat on the couch with his grandmother, Minho firmly ensconced between them. The dog's head lay in Tam's lap. When Soo entered the room, Minho looked up, wagged his tail, then dropped his head, licked his chops, and yawned.

"Okay, you two," Soo said, referring to her son and Minho. "Time for bed."

"Oh, come on, Mom," Tam complained. "Just a few more minutes?"

Soo sat in her easy chair beside the couch. "Five minutes, then it's lights out."

"Fifteen."

"*Ten.*"

Tam smiled. "Deal."

Soo shook her head. Their playful negotiation for extended television viewing time had been a game she had been playing with her son for as long as she could remember.

Minho fell asleep and began snoring.

"Did you send the request?" Soo's mother asked.

Soo nodded, put a finger to her lips.

Her mother nodded.

"What request?" Tam asked.

"Nothing, honey," Soo replied. "Just work-related stuff."

"Like what?"

"You know I can't talk about my job, Tam."

Tam nodded. "I know. National security... top secret... blah, blah, blah."

Soo smiled. "Exactly."

"But you told Gran?"

"I told Gran I had to send an email before I went to bed."

"But she said *request*."

"So?"

"That would imply that she knew what the subject of the email was about."

Soo smiled. "Do you have any idea how hard it is having a genius for a son?"

Tam rolled his eyes. "Do you have any idea how hard it is *being* a genius?"

Soo laughed. "I'll give you that one. Five minutes."

Minho lifted his tail, raised his head, sniffed the air, then jumped down from the couch.

Tam scrunched up his face. "Ewww! Minho! That was gross!"

The dog sat on the floor across from his master. He appeared to be smiling.

"That's gotta be one of your worst farts ever!" Tam exclaimed.

Minho yawned and wagged his tail.

"On that pleasant note, time's up," Soo said. "Both of you upstairs to bed. Now."

Tam gave his mother and grandmother a goodnight kiss, then spoke to Minho. "Come on, gas bag. Bedtime."

The dog trotted behind his master, then ran up the stairs ahead of him.

Tam called out. "Don't even think about sleeping on the bed, stink butt!"

Soo walked to the kitchen table, picked up the listening device, returned to the living room, sat on the couch beside her mother, held it between her fingers, and spoke to it. "It's late, Mom. I'm going to pass on watching TV. You can stay up if you'd like but, I'm turning in."

"Good idea," Soo's mother said.

Soo stood, turned off the television and the lights. The two women walked to the living room window. Soo parted the drapes, peeked outside.

The car parked down the street started up, then drove past their house.

Soo glanced at the listening device she held in her hand, watched as its tiny power indicator light went out.

Someone had turned it off.

16

___

Chili And Beans

SENIOR FIRST OFFICER Galloway exited the flight deck, passed Jules and Rigor, who lay fast asleep in their hammocks, tapped Matt on his shoulder.

Matt came around slowly. "What's up?"

"Captain Arden asked me to tell you we'll be crossing into Russian airspace in two hours. If your team needs to get squared away, now would be the time to do it."

Matt rolled his head left, right, cracked his neck. "Copy that."

The SFO nodded, took his leave, returned to the cockpit, closed the door.

Matt put his arm around Kyla, kissed her neck. "Rise and shine," he said. "It's almost showtime."

Kyla moaned her objection to being awakened. "Noooo!"

"Let's go," Matt said. "Up and at 'em."

"I want pancakes."

"Sorry, no pancakes on this flight."

"With scrambled eggs…"

"That I can do. The eggs are dehydrated. Boil-in-bag packets are at the front of the plane."

"And bacon… smothered in butter and syrup."

Matt smiled. "Now you're making me hungry."

Kyla opened her eyes, stared at Matt. "*Pleaassee*?"

"Tell you what," Matt replied. "I'll make you breakfast in bed when we get back home. I'll even throw in a glass of freshly squeezed orange juice."

Kyla pouted, rolled out of the hammock. "You better!"

Matt walked up the plane to the hammocks in which Jules and Rigor slept, gently nudged Jules's shoulder. She opened her eyes. "Everything okay, Matt?"

Matt nodded, glanced at Rigor. "We're two hours out. Wake up Sleeping Beauty and grab some chow. I want to go over everything one last time before we gear up for the drop."

Jules stretched. "Copy that."

Matt walked to the food station, opened a packet of instant coffee, poured the contents into a mug, added hot water from the dispenser, sipped the beverage. The robust blend was strong, hit the spot.

Rigor awoke to the smell of the coffee. "Mmm, good. Me. Want. Coffee."

Matt smiled. "How do you take it?"

Rigor rolled out of his hammock, hit the floor, and immediately launched into a pushup workout. "Black," he grunted.

Matt looked at Jules as he made Rigor's coffee, shook his head.

"It's his normal morning routine," Jules explained on Rigor's behalf. "One hundred pushups, followed by one hundred sit-ups, a quick swim in the ocean, then breakfast."

Kyla joined Matt at the self-serve food station, waited for him to make her a cup of coffee.

Matt set Rigor's coffee on the station. "It's ready when you are, Rig."

"Thanks, boss," Rigor replied between breaths.

Kyla took the hot coffee Matt had prepared for her, sipped it. "Mmm," she said. "Good."

"Listen up," Matt said. "We're two hours from Russian airspace, which means we'll HALO out five minutes before that. Captain Arden has our drop coordinates. He'll put us on target."

"And when we get there?" Rigor asked as he jumped to his feet.

"Cross provided me with a ground contact. He'll meet us at the drop zone and transport us from there to Vladivostok."

Rigor nodded. "Copy that." He rifled through the ready-to-eat meal packets, selected one. "Chili and beans," he said. "Awesome!"

"You're going to eat that for *breakfast*?" Jules asked.

"You check out the macros in this puppy?" Rigor said. "Twelve hundred calories. That'll provide enough energy exchange to take me through until lunch." He selected a second packet, shoved it in his pocket. "Spaghetti with meat-balls! Excellent!"

"Rigor has a point," Matt said. "Everyone grab extra rations. Store them inside your drop suit. I'm sure we won't be waiting long for pick up, but it's best to be prepared just in case. I need to make a phone call. Rig, run down the gear with Kyla and Jules again. Make sure they're as familiar with it as you are."

"You've got it," Rigor replied as he tore into the packet of chili and beans. "But first, brekkie."

Matt walked to his bag, removed the satellite phone he had taken from the hangar, then headed to the rear of the plane to make the call in private. He sat in a fold-down chair, dialed the number Task Force Chief Cross had given him for Alexander Kurien.

The phone rang, the call connected. "This is Kurien."

The man's accent was more American than Russian.

Matt spoke the code phrase he had been instructed to say upon making first contact with the former CIA counter-intelligence officer turned businessman. "Falcon is circling."

Silence followed Matt's words. Finally, Kurien spoke. "I've been expecting your call, Reaper. How may I help you?"

17

No Choice

D R. JIN CHO tossed in her sleep, bothered once more by the same disturbing dream. She knew she was not to blame for what she had done. In fact, she had not been given a choice.

Last week, she had been shopping for a birthday gift for her colleague's son, Tam, when two men approached her and ordered her to come with them. She objected at first but offered no further resistance when they presented their credentials, informed her they were agents of the Reconnaissance General Bureau assigned to Nest 5, and informed her that the matter had to do with national security. She remembered the feeling of her blood suddenly rushing from her head to her feet, and the chill that rippled over her body. She had heard of such instances occurring in the past. State workers, abducted off the street by government agents, were never to be seen or heard from again. But she was no ordinary state worker. She was assigned to the most secret scientific project ever to have been undertaken in the RGB's Organic Warfare & Containment facility, of which she was the co-lead researcher. Together with her research partner, Dr. Soo Park, she had developed a revolutionary nano-particulate chemical nerve agent, Synoxin-9, the details of which they would be presenting in just a few days at a closed-door conference in Vladivostok. The two men had escorted her out of the shopping mall and ushered her into a waiting sedan as passersby looked on. For the next hour, they briefed her on the observe-and-report assignment she was being ordered to carry out. They rifled through her purchases, tossed aside the casual dress, shoes, and LEGOs she had bought, pulled out the small stuffed raccoon squeaky toy, and asked her why she had purchased it. She explained it was an additional gift to the LEGOs which were Tam's birthday present. The plush raccoon was an inexpensive gift for his dog, Minho.

She awoke in a cold sweat, bolted upright in bed, took a second to get her bearings in the darkness, then left her bed, walked to the bedroom window, and looked outside.

The street was empty of pedestrians and parked cars.

Unlike last night.

She thought she had recognized the two men seated in the car parked down the street from her home as the same RGB agents who had escorted her out of the mall and subsequently assigned her to question Dr. Park about her brother. They had wanted to know how close the two were and if he had reached out to her since his escape from North Korea. She had told them theirs was a professional working relationship and not a personal one. When pressed as to why she would buy a gift for Dr. Park's son if they were not friends, she explained she wanted to do it as a gesture of kindness because she knew Soo was hurting. She had seen a change in her disposition and performance in the lab since her brother had disappeared without a trace. She had become distant and empty. Soo never spoke of her social life, and Jin suspected this was because she had no one else in her life, save for her mother, son, and dog. The sudden death of Soo's husband had nearly destroyed her. It was human compassion that had led her to buy the gift and the toy, plain and simple.

The younger of the two agents left the room with the toy, returned twenty minutes later, handed it to her, and told her exactly what she was to do. Too frightened to ask questions, Jin nodded and agreed to deliver the gifts to Soo at the lab the next day, per their instructions.

The older agent pressed her for the next ten minutes. He ended their conversation by warning her that should it later be discovered she had neglected to disclose any important information to them that was relative to her relationship with Dr. Park, or her knowledge of her brother's where-abouts, she would be arrested. She assured them she had told them all she knew and asked if she could leave. The interrogation now complete, the agents returned her to the shopping mall.

Jin glanced at the clock on her nightstand. The numbers on the LED display glowed bright red. The time: 12:45 A.M.

She would have to be up in five hours to get herself ready for work and meet the bus outside her door, which would transport her to Nest 5. She thought of its blacked-out windows and the black sack they would place over her head the second she was seated, which would prevent her from seeing where she was going. The RGB's security protocol was grossly disrespectful of such high-profile citizens such as herself. In Jin's opinion, it bordered on inhumane. Regardless, she knew better than to voice her objection.

The gunshot she had heard once before, after the bus had pulled off to the side of the road, still rang in her ears. She had wanted to remove her hood at that moment, run out of the bus, and keep running, to get as far away from her life as possible. But fear held her in her seat. Had she run, she would be the next to die. As fast a runner as she might be, she could never outrun a bullet.

The clock display flashed again: 12:46 A.M.

Jin returned to her bed, pulled the covers up to her neck, nestled in under the sheets, and closed her eyes. She tried to put the dream out of her mind.

Tomorrow would be a new and better day.

Or so she hoped.

18

Alexander Kurien

THE FORMER CIA officer turned businessman broke the ice with Matt. "So, Reaper," he asked. "How's the old man doing, anyway? Still as feisty as ever?"

Matt liked him. "Yes, sir."

Alexander Kurien laughed. "That is one tough son of a bitch. Being trained by him was like walking through a house of fire every day. Doesn't surprise me one bit that he made Task Force Chief."

"TFC Cross has had a very successful career with the agency," Matt replied. "I can't think of anyone better suited to run the Special Operations Group than him."

"I couldn't agree more," Kurien said. "The man has more experience in executing and running tactical paramilitary and clandestine covert operations than anyone I know. Word is even the president considers him a legend. How many other agency brass do you know who have a standing invitation to golf with the president?"

Matt smiled. "None, sir."

"Cross must consider you to be one hell of an operative if he's put you in command of your own unit, Reaper."

"It's my honor to serve, sir."

"Yes, son, it is. Anyway, enough with the chin wagging. I have two questions for you. What do you need from me, and how soon do you need it?"

"Covert transportation," Matt replied, "and emergency exfil, should we require it."

"Done. Transpo from where to where?"

"The Livandyskay mountain range to Vladivostok. We'll be dropping into Russian airspace two hours from now."

"Dropping in?"

"Via HALO."

"Hmm," Kurien replied. "That's a gutsy move. The Livandyskay range is heavily patrolled by Russian ground forces. They use it for extreme conditions training. You could run into problems there, so watch your six. Take my word for it. Trouble with them isn't something you want."

"Copy that. The mountains are our only option. Our timeline is too tight to infiltrate the country by any other means. We'll have darkness on our side. Plus, there's no moon tonight."

"I assume you'll be armed?"

"Yes, sir. Small arms and MK18s, both fitted with suppressors."

"Send me your GPS coordinates when you're on the

ground. I'm in Khabarovsk now. It's a short flight to Vladi-vostok. I have an office there and the proper transportation to suit your needs. There's a sightseeing road that winds through the mountains. It's well marked, so you can't miss it. Find it, drop me a pin, then sit tight. I'll be driving a blacked-out Lincoln Navigator with diplomatic plates. The plates were a present from one of my clients, whose ass I saved. I can drive it anywhere in Russia and never be stopped by the authorities. I'll take you and your team straight to your hotel. Where are you staying?"

"The Grand."

"First class all the way."

"It's more of a requirement, actually."

"Proximity to the target?"

"Correct."

"If you need additional fingers on triggers, I can provide them. My men are the best in Russia."

"No thanks, sir," Matt replied. "This is a black op which has been sanctioned at the highest level. You know what that means."

"That Cross will be providing POTUS with mission updates as soon as you send them."

"Precisely. You're the only one who'll know who we really are. As far as everyone else is concerned, we're just four American businesspeople visiting Vladivostok."

"Sounds good. I'd like to do you a favor if you'll permit me."

"What's that?"

"A close friend of mine owns The Grand. I'll make a call and move your team to the twentieth floor, which is off limits to all but authorized guests. It has a private elevator, plus the windows are bulletproof. It's reserved for use by dignitaries and oligarchs when they're in town. Say the word and it's yours."

"That would be appreciated. Thank you."

"Thank Cross when you're back stateside. I wouldn't be in the position I'm in now, were it not for Cameron. TFC Cross may be your boss, but he's my friend."

"Sounds like he made the right call when he reached out to you for support."

"Damn right he did. I'd take a bullet for that man in a heartbeat."

"Copy that."

"Where are you taking your HVA once you're out of Vladivostok?"

"An agency black site in Seoul."

"Just how high value is this high value asset?"

"The highest."

"To the Russians as well?"

"To any government on Earth with a military."

"Then know that if the Russians choose to pursue you, they'll shut everything down. Airports, roadways, trains, you name it. You'll wish you could *teleport* to Seoul, but don't worry. I've got you covered."

"How's that, sir?" Matt asked.

"How do you feel about yachts?"

"That it will be too slow a means of exfil if we've got the Russian military on our asses."

"Normally, that would be true. But you don't know my yacht."

"Sir?"

Kurien paused. "You trust me, son?"

"I do."

"Good. You should. I'll get you and your people out of the country. Most importantly, no one will even know you left Russia."

"Sounds like a plan," Matt replied.

19

Blame Mom

SOO ROSE EARLY, showered, slipped into her housecoat, then checked her computer. She had hoped to have received an email confirming that Tam would be permitted to accompany her on her trip to Vladivostok, but her inbox was empty. The more she thought about it, the more she realized that she was getting ahead of herself. Such a request would have to be run up the chain of command. The reality was that her request might very well have been dismissed by administrative higher-ups upon receipt, and that she might not receive a reply at all. With any luck, that wouldn't be the case. She had made a very good case for Tam in her request, citing his being in the top half of one percent in academic standing in all of North Korea, and that spotlighting him as the face of North Korea's next generation of super youths would reflect well not just on the country, but on the Supreme Leader himself. She watched the screen impatiently for another minute, then left the machine, walked to Tam's room, opened his door, and looked in. The boy was still asleep, half his blankets thrown off the bed and on the floor. She smiled and wondered how it was possible that he could wake up in such a disheveled bed every morning yet never complain about having had a bad night's sleep. Minho lifted his head off the bed, saw Soo standing in the doorway, slapped his tail against Tam's headboard. Soo raised a finger to her lips, shushed the dog. Minho dropped his tail, yawned, plopped his head back down on his master's chest, let out a heavy sigh, then fell back to sleep. Soo closed the door and headed downstairs to make breakfast for her family.

She flicked on the kitchen lights, crossed the room, walked to the front window, looked outside. It was still dark. The surveillance vehicle that she and her mother had seen parked on the street for the last two days was not there. This was a good thing. It informed her that she was not under twenty-four-hour surveillance. The listening device sat on the end table beside the couch, its power indicator light still off. She picked up the bug and placed it on a bookshelf across from the couch. From there, she and her mother could keep an eye on it and see when its power light turned on. She would have to find a way to tell Tam what was going on and to make up some excuse that he would believe for why their family's home had been bugged in such a manner. He was smart, and Soo had always found that treating him like an adult rather than a child yielded the most successful results. He had been raised to know he was intellectually gifted, far and above any of his schoolmates. Soo and her late husband had also instructed him that he was not to abuse his gift by slighting others who were not his equal. He was turning out to be a fine young man who would soon find his place in the world. Presenting his skills in some small way at the conference in Vladivostok could be an important moment in his life.

Soo opened the cupboard door above the stove, removed a box of pancake mix and a bottle of syrup. She added the mix and water to a bowl, walked to the refrigerator, withdrew a carton of eggs, then heard her mother's footsteps coming down the stairs. Without saying a word, her mother took her place in the morning assembly line, retrieved a frying pan from a cupboard beneath the countertop, coated the bottom of the pan with butter, placed it atop the stove, and turned on the burner.

"What's your preference this morning, daughter?" she asked. "Scrambled or fried?"

A voice called out from the second floor. "Scrambled."

Soo turned to her mother and smiled. "I swear that boy has bionic hearing."

Her mother nodded. "Would it surprise you to learn he did?"

Soo laughed. "As a matter of fact, it wouldn't."

Tam called out again. "Minho is asking for pancakes, too."

"Minho is *not* having pancakes," Soo replied. "Not unless you want Gran to put you on after-school diarrhea poop detail. And you know she will!"

"Eww, Mom," Tam replied. "Gross!"

Soo heard Tam talking to his dog. "Sorry, Minho. No pancakes for you."

Minho mewled his displeasure at being denied the breakfast treat.

"Hey, it's not my fault," Tam said as he bounded down the stairs and entered the kitchen with the dog on his heels. "Blame mom."

"Sure," Soo said. "Throw *me* under the bus."

Tam smiled mischievously.

"You hungry?" Soo asked.

"Starving!" Tam replied.

"Great. That means you're in charge of making the pancakes while I dress for work." She handed Tam a wire whisk. "Instructions are on the back of the box." She tousled her son's hair. "Be sure to make them nice and fluffy."

Tam groaned. "Ah, come on, Mom. Can't I just play video games instead?"

Gran interjected. "Sure."

"Awesome!"

"Just know it's hard to eat a video game."

"Huh?"

"Would you prefer a nice hot breakfast of pancakes, eggs, and juice or playing video games?"

"Can't I have both?"

"Not in this house, grandson," Gran replied. "Here we pull our own weight, so start mixing."

Soo laughed. "You're outnumbered, buddy. I suggest you get a move on."

Tam walked to the counter, read the preparation instructions on the box, filled the measuring cup with water, added the pancake mix, began stirring. "Not fair," he said.

"Life's not fair, Tam," Gran replied. She nudged her grandson playfully. "Get used to it."

Minho sat beside Tam, eager to snag any morsel that might fall on the floor.

"Forget it, fart bag," Tam said. "Cleaning up your regular poop is bad enough, never mind diarrhea poop!"

Soo dressed, applied her makeup, checked her email one last time before heading downstairs to join her family for breakfast. She was shocked when she read the subject line of the only message in her inbox: YOUR REQUEST HAS BEEN GRANTED.

20

Into The Darkness

MATT BROUGHT HIS team up to speed on his conversation with Alexander Kurien. "Cross's contact is making himself available to us for whatever we need, including exfil from Vladivostok."

"Do we have a rally point?" Kyla asked.

"Not yet," Matt replied. "I'll send him our coordinates when we're on the ground. He mentioned a scenic road which runs through the Livandyskays. We're to take cover in the forest and wait for him to arrive."

"Who is this guy?" Rigor asked.

"His name is Alexander Kurien," Matt replied. "He used to be one of us. Now he's gone private. He's the go-to guy in Russian for private security."

"In other words, he's a glorified bodyguard," Jules said.

Matt shook his head. "He's a former field operative now

in charge of a team of highly trained operatives. Don't downplay his importance because he's a private contractor."

"I'll ask him for his card," Rigor said. "Who knows? I might just hit him up for a job one day."

Matt smiled. "Forget it. You're going to have your hands full with NOMAD. Unless, of course, you prefer the cold of Russia to the warmth of the Caribbean."

Rigor replied. "Thanks for shattering my dreams of rubbing shoulders with millionaires and oligarchs."

"I don't think so, scuba boy," Jules said. "Oligarchs, smoligarchs. There's no way I'd ever move to Russia. And if you think I'd let you go there on your own, you're out of your mind."

Rigor turned to Kyla and winked. "See what I put up with? The woman has no sense of adventure."

"She's a trained CIA operative who is about to jump out of a commercial aircraft and parachute to the ground in the dark," Kyla replied. "It doesn't get more adventurous than that!"

Jules smiled. "Thank you, Kyla."

Kyla nodded. "No worries, sister. I've got you."

"Uh-oh," Rigor said.

"What is it?" Matt asked.

"We're in trouble."

"How so?"

"They're bonding."

Kyla put her arm around Jules. "Damn right we are."

"Good," Matt replied. "This team needs to be tight. Once we exit this aircraft, we need to function as one entity. If I say go left, we go left. Right, we go right. Under no circumstances do we operate independently unless the situation demands it, and even then we make every attempt to regroup as soon as possible. Everyone got that?"

The team nodded.

"Don't worry, boss," Rigor said. "We've got this."

"We need to have each other's backs down there," Matt said. "This is our first mission as a new team. I don't need to remind you how important it is that it goes off as planned."

The captain made an announcement over the intercom. His voice boomed throughout the hollow fuselage. "Ten minutes to drop. Gear up and watch for my green."

Matt called out. "Copy that." He addressed his team. "Showtime. Suit up. Anyone need to go over our HALO drop one last time?"

"Personally," Kyla said, "I could have done without Rigor's human pancake reference. That's the last thing I want going through my mind as I'm dropping through the sky."

"To be accurate," Rigor replied, "mess up this jump and the last thing that will be going through your mind will be your feet."

Kyla shook her head. "Thanks for the visual."

Rigor grinned widely. "You're welcome."

Matt stepped into his HALO suit, geared up, fitted his oxygen mask to his face, double-checked its seal, ensuring it was tight. He slipped on his parachute, fitted it to his body. He pulled off the mask, addressed the team. "Rigor," he said. "Weapons."

"Copy that," Rigor said. He stepped away from the group, opened the tactical bags lying on the floor of the aircraft, pulled out four MK18 assault rifles and extra magazines, handed them out.

Matt took the weapon, inserted the magazine, made it

mission ready, slung it over his body, secured it close to his chest. He slipped on his backpack, tactical gloves, and helmet, then checked the operability of the night vision system attached to his helmet. It worked perfectly. "Everyone ready?" he asked.

Rigor, Jules, and Kyla gave him a thumbs up.

The captain spoke again. "One minute to drop," he announced. "Opening the compartment now. Take your positions and go on my green."

The team moved forward, entered the drop bay, fitted their oxygen masks in place, waited.

The red light which illuminated the drop bay turned green.

Matt held Kyla's hand.

Rigor held Jules's.

Together they jumped out of the A350 and plummeted down, down, down through the pre-dawn darkness.

21

Amazing News

SOO WAS SO excited she could hardly contain herself. She rushed down the stairs, a printout of the email she had just received in her hand. "I have amazing news!" she announced.

Tam sat at the breakfast table with Minho at his feet. The dog smelled the pancakes and eggs and pawed at his master's leg, hoping to receive a bite of the delicious meal. Tam looked down at the dog. "Forget it, fart bag. Mom will kill me. I'll feed you in a few minutes."

Minho dropped his paw. Undaunted, he raised it a few seconds later and waved it in the air for attention.

"Knock it off, mooch," Tam said.

Soo's mother spoke. "What news is that, honey?"

"I didn't think they'd allow it, but they did!" Soo replied.

Gran shrugged. "Who are *they,* and what did they allow?"

"I sent a request to the Reconnaissance General Bureau asking if it would be possible for Tam to attend the Russian conference with me."

"And they said yes?"

"More than that," Soo exclaimed. "They approved everyone. We're all going to Vladivostok!"

Gran plated her and Soo's breakfast and returned the hot skillet to the stovetop. "Are you serious?"

Soo nodded. "The approval came from the office of the Supreme Leader himself."

"Are you sure it's not a mistake?" Gran asked.

Soo shook her head. "The RGB would never make a mistake like this. There are channels a request like this has to go through. It's one hundred percent legitimate."

"That's incredible honey," Gran said. "But you and Tam go. I'll stay home with Minho. You can tell me all about it when you get back."

"I can't do that, Mom," Soo objected.

"Why not?"

"Do you realize how much of an honor this is? Not having my family with me at the conference after the invitation has been extended would be an insult to the Supreme Leader. You have to come. If you don't, who knows what repercussions could be leveled against me in the future? I might even lose my job."

Tam interjected. "But if we're all going, who's gonna take care of Minho? We can't leave him here on his own."

Soo smiled. "Well, the email says the invitation has been extended to us as a family. Minho's part of our family, right?"

Tam's face brightened. "Are you saying he can come with us?"

Soo nodded. "I don't see why not."

"Cool!" Tam exclaimed. He looked down at the dog. "You hear that, boy? You're coming with us to Russia!"

Minho cocked his head and whined. He was sure the elation in his master's voice meant that he was one second closer to receiving a forkful of pancakes drizzled with syrup.

"When do we leave?" her mother asked.

"Tomorrow," Soo said. "I've been instructed to wrap up my lab work today. Tomorrow will be a travel day. The conference takes place on the following day."

"That doesn't give us much time to get ready."

Soo shook her head. "No, it doesn't. I was expecting to be the only one going. Now we'll have to hustle. And I have to work today."

"Never mind, sweetheart," Gran said. "Don't worry about a thing. Have breakfast and go to work. I'll get Tam off to school. We're only away for a couple of days so we can pack light, right?"

Soo nodded. "I'm sure a change of clothes and toiletries is all we'll need."

"Then leave everything to me. I'll pack for everyone, including Minho."

Soo kissed her mother's cheek. "Thanks, Mom," she said. "You're the best."

Her mother beamed. "Yes, I am."

22

Three Minutes

ATT HEARD RIGOR'S voice through his helmet's communications system as he and his team plummeted down through the predawn sky. Through his night vision goggles, the Livandyskay mountain range drew closer with every passing second. "Comm's check," Rigor said. "How's everybody doing so far?"

"Good," Matt replied. "Kyla... Jules... report."

"I left my stomach behind when we jumped," Jules said. "Guess there's no chance I can go back for it, huh?"

There was a smile in Rigor's voice. "Fraid not, beautiful." He glanced at Jules, squeezed her hand. "You're doing fine. Remember, as long as you don't panic, there's nothing to be afraid of."

"Say's the guy who made a point of scaring the crap out of us with his pancake landing jokes," Kyla replied.

"You good, Kyla?" Matt asked.

Kyla glanced at him. "Surprisingly, yes."

Matt spoke to Rigor. "What's our drop time?"

"Three minutes," Rigor said. "I suggest everyone get comfortable and enjoy the view."

"*Three minutes?*" Jules said. "From forty-three thousand feet? Just how fast are we falling?"

"We've already reached terminal velocity," Rigor replied. "Our current rate of descent is two hundred miles per hour."

"Holy shit!" Jules said.

"When do we deploy?" Kyla asked.

"When we reach one thousand feet," Rigor replied. "The closer we get to the ground, the faster it will appear to be rushing up at us. You'll need to listen to me carefully. When I tell you to pull your rip cord, pull it. Not a second before or later. Everybody got that?"

"Copy that," Matt said.

"Mind if I offer a suggestion, Matt?" Jules asked.

"Sure," Matt replied.

"Next time, before you settle on a nighttime HALO jump as a means of infiltration, realize that it is a horrible idea and come up with a different plan."

Matt smiled. "I'll take that under advisement."

"Two minutes to deployment," Rigor announced. "Gauge check. How's everyone's oxygen?"

"I'm good," Jules replied.

"Same," Kyla added.

"Good to go," Matt said.

"For HALO rookies, you guys are doing all right," Rigor

said. "I would have expected at least one of you to be redlining by now."

"Redlining?" Kyla asked.

"To have almost sucked your oxygen supply dry."

"People do that?" Jules asked.

"It's been known to happen."

"And what happens when they do?"

"They pass out from oxygen deprivation. Unless someone can navigate to them through the air, hook up to them, then tandem with them to the ground, they'll be unable to self-deploy. And we all know by now how that can end, don't we?"

Matt, Kyla, and Jules spoke in unison. "Pancake city."

There was a smile in Rigor's voice. "You guys catch on fast." He paused. "Sixty seconds to deployment."

The Livandyskay mountain range seemed to double in size with each additional second of freefall.

"All of us have jumped before as part of our training, but from lower altitudes," Rigor said. "HALO is different. Falling at this speed and deploying at one thousand feet will feel like it's too late. You'll need to fight the urge to pull your chute before then. Don't worry. We're packing fast-opening military-grade canopies. They've been designed for that very purpose: to open quickly and give you total control over your landing. As soon as your chute opens, it'll pull you back up into the sky. That's normal. With these chutes, it'll happen faster. Be ready for it. Twenty seconds."

"Rigor," Matt asked. "Check your three o'clock."

Rigor looked to his right. "Shit!" he replied. "We've got company."

"Looks like Russian ground forces on patrol in the region," Matt said. "I make three in the convoy. You?"

"Yeah."

"We need to touch down as far away from them as possible."

"Copy that," Rigor replied. "Okay, kids. Listen up. New plan. Lean into the freefall and follow me down."

"What about deploying at one thousand feet?" Jules asked.

Rigor pointed. "See that opening in the forest? If we can make it there, we'll land out of sight of the convoy. To do that, we'll need to rip at eight hundred feet, not one thousand."

"Eight hundred feet?" Jules said. "Are you freaking kidding me? Do you know how close to the ground that is?"

"Remember what I said. You panic, you die. Personally, I've rather enjoyed our time together so far. It would be nice to keep the band together a little longer."

"Do we have a choi—?"

"*Now!*" Rigor yelled. "*Pull, pull, pull!*"

The team yanked on their ripcords, felt the sudden jolt in their harnesses as their chutes deployed, pulling them skyward. They continued to descend, pulling left and right on their directional control cords as they skimmed over the treetops. Seconds later, they safely reached the ground.

One by one, they ran ahead as their feet touched the ground, stopping as their parachutes fell feather-light to the ground behind them.

The team quickly unbuckled their harnesses and freed themselves from their gear.

Matt called out. "Everybody okay?"

Jules replied. "Okay? Yes. Do I want to repeat that little stunt anytime soon? Hell, no!"

"You did great, sweetheart," Rigor said as he gathered his chute from the ground. "I'm proud of you."

"Compliment me all you want," Jules said. "Next time I'm flying commercial."

"Oh, come on," Rigor replied. "Where's the fun in that?"

"I'm with Jules," Kyla said.

Rigor looked at Matt, raised his hands. "There they go again with that whole bonding thing. I tell you, buddy, pretty soon we'll be on our own. It'll be us against—"

Matt raised his arm, made a fist, dropped to one knee.

The team knelt in unison, fell silent.

Matt pointed. "Get behind the tree line. Move!"

Rigor, Kyla, and Jules gathered their gear and followed Matt out of the clearing and deep into the forest. They took cover, watched, listened.

Truck engines revved in the distance. Sabers of bright light slashed through the trees at harsh angles, rising and falling in the inky darkness.

"The Russian patrol," Rigor whispered.

Matt nodded. He raised his rifle, pointed it toward the beams of light as they danced in the distance. "Kyla and Jules," he ordered. "Move southeast, slowly and quietly. Stay low and out of sight. Establish a perimeter. Rigor, you're with me. Everyone stay on comms and watch your crossfire."

"You plan on engaging with them?" Rigor asked.

"Not if I don't have to," Matt replied. "But if it comes down to it, only one team will leave this mountain alive. And it won't be them."

23

I Know What You Did

SOO ARRIVED AT Nest 5's secret location, took the elevator up one floor to her lab, carded in, changed out of her street clothes into her protective lab attire, then passed through the airlock and settled in at her workstation. She began pouring through the computer files she would require for the conference in Vladivostok.

Jin arrived moments later. The airlock hissed as the door's rubber bladder automatically sealed itself shut behind her. She entered the lab, saw Soo sitting at her computer, felt an air of tension in the room. She broke the uneasy silence. "You have a good night?" she asked.

Soo kept her head down, continued reviewing the files on her computer. "It was quiet," she replied.

"How's your mother and Tam?"

"Fine."

"Minho?"

"Fine."

"Does Minho like the toy I bought him?"

Soo stopped what she was doing. She wanted to confront Jin about the toy, ask her how the listening device ended up in the plush raccoon, how long she had been working with the RGB behind her back, and what her motive was. Instead, she reminded herself that the lab was under constant audio and visual surveillance. Perhaps Jin's question was as innocent as she had intended it to be, or perhaps it wasn't. She smiled politely. "He loves it," she replied.

"I'm glad," Jin said. "Tam's lucky to have him. I'm sure they're great company for one another."

"Tam has his grandmother too, Jin. And me."

"I just meant that since your husband passed away, Tam is fortunate that Minho is there to—"

Soo cut her off mid-sentence. "We present our research on Synoxin-9 in two days. That should be the focus of our discussion right now."

Jin picked up on the curtness in Soo's voice. "Of course."

"We'll break it down into two parts," Soo said. "I'll start and you'll follow. We'll close together. My presentation will focus on the toxin's biochemistry and chemical composition. You'll explain its mechanism of delivery and dispersion."

Jin was not happy. "Delivery and dispersion? That's it?"

"Yes," Soo said. "I'll present the hard science behind the development of Synoxin-9 and its application as a smart bioweapon. You can discuss its payload integration with nuclear warheads, drones, and the like."

"This was supposed to be an opportunity for both of us to shine in front of our Supreme Leader," Jin said curtly.

"It will be."

"Not if you steal the spotlight, it won't."

"There is no spotlight to steal, Jin. Our work has your name on it too."

"You know the way these conferences work," Jin argued. "The delegates might be listening with their ears, but they'll be remembering with their eyes. They'll see you as the scientist who developed Synoxin-9. There will be no *us*. I'll be seen as nothing more than your sidekick."

"Need I remind you who was named lead scientist on this project?" Soo said bluntly. "Me, Jin. Not you. Don't think I haven't felt your animosity about that since day one. We were assigned to work together on this project by senior officials within the RGB. I never requested you, just like you never requested me. Designing this toxin was our job. We accomplished what our government ordered us to do. Are you going to let your bruised ego affect the quality of our presentation? Do you know what would happen to you if you did?"

Jin fell silent.

"I'll tell you," Soo continued. "Not only would you be removed from this project, but you'd also be removed from all future Nest projects as well. You'd never work for the State again. You and your family would lose your beautiful home and be sent to social housing. You'd be assigned to work in a nondescript lab on unimportant projects. Is that what you want?"

Jin considered her response. "No."

"Good. Now go to your workstation, finish your presentation, and copy me on your notes. This discussion has been a waste of my time. I don't plan to waste any more on it."

Jin acquiesced. "As you wish. It's your show."

"One last thing," Soo said.

"What?" Jin replied curtly.

Soo leaned in, whispered in her ear. There was anger in her voice. "I found the bug."

Jin felt the blood rush out of her face.

She turned and walked away.

24

Stolichnaya

ATT MOTIONED TO Rigor, made a chopping signal with his hand. Rigor nodded, then moved quickly through the forest in the direction Matt had indicated, keeping his eyes on both the rough terrain underfoot and the approaching Russian military patrol. Three figures emerged from the opposite side of the open field in which they had landed. The men moved slowly; their rifles pointed into the darkness.

Matt whispered to his team through his comms mic. "They're conducting a sweep. Maintain a three-sixty visual. If they've called for additional support we'll have a problem, so stay sharp. We're surrounded by forest and don't know where we are. They have home field advantage."

"If we take them now, we can use their vehicles," Kyla said.

"Negative," Matt replied. "If we can avoid a firefight, we will. We'll hold for the moment and see where this goes."

The three soldiers who had entered the field were soon joined by additional members of their patrol. The heavily armed Russian militia met in the middle of the field, turned off the flashlights affixed to their rifles, and began talking. Laughter followed. They were soon joined by three more of their comrades. One of the men yelled out to the others. His announcement was met with a loud cheer.

Matt removed his night vision monocular from his jumpsuit, turned it on, spied on the group. He focused the device on the loud man, then spoke to his team. "He has a bottle in his hand. Looks like they're not after us after all."

"Which means they didn't see us land," Rigor replied. "Could be the topography of the region. They could have been traveling uphill. The trees must have blocked their view of us when we hit eight hundred feet."

"Copy that," Matt said.

"This field must be where they sneak off to have a few drinks while they're out on patrol," Jules said. "If we'd landed here a minute later, we'd have crashed their party."

"Yeah," Kyla added. "And something tells me that wouldn't have ended well. For us, I mean."

"We'll wait it out," Matt said. "Stay quiet. Let's not give them any reason to suspect we're here."

The men joked with one another as they passed the bottle back and forth, each taking a hearty swig. The loud man removed a packet of cigarettes from his jacket pocket, offered his comrades a smoke, struck up a match, and lit their cigarettes.

"Nasty habit," Rigor whispered as he observed the group through his monocular. "Those cancer sticks will kill you.

However, I recognize the brand of vodka they're drinking. Stolichnaya. Good choice."

The men strolled about the field, drinking and smoking. The loud man raised the bottle to his mouth, drank the last of the liquor, then broke away from the group.

He was headed in Kyla's direction.

Kyla watched him approach. "Shit," she said.

"Stay calm," Matt said. He raised his rifle, scoped him, placed the weapon's crosshairs in the middle of the soldier's forehead. "I have him, Kyla. If I think you're in trouble, I'll put him down."

"Copy that," Kyla whispered.

"I have eyes on the secondary targets," Rigor said. "Awaiting your go."

"Same here," Jules said.

"Hold," Matt said. "Let's see what he's up to first."

"Copy," Rigor replied.

The Russian reached the edge of the forest.

Kyla lay on her stomach, ten feet from the soldier, her finger on the trigger of her weapon. Her dark green and black camouflage jumpsuit made her impossible to see against the dark forest floor.

She watched as the soldier raised his arms, then slipped the mouth of the empty vodka bottle over an overhanging tree branch. The branch sagged under its weight. Kyla looked up. The bottle hung three feet above her head. She watched as the soldier walked back to his comrades, called out to them, and pointed.

Jules understood what the man said. "Fuck!" she said.

"What is it?" Kyla said.

"Kyla," Jules said. "Lay as flat on the ground as you can. Use every inch of that tree trunk for cover. Copy?"

"Why?" Kyla asked as she complied with Jules' request. "What's happening?"

Jules replied. "You're about to come under fi—"

Matt watched as the loud man stepped aside, invited the men to fire their weapons. One by one they aimed at the swaying vodka bottle and shot, sending round after round whizzing through the forest. Five shots later, the bottle shattered to pieces. Glass fragments rained down over Kyla, covered her head and back. A loud cheer emanated from the group as the branch which had supported the empty bottle broke off the tree and fell, an innocent victim of the gunfire.

The men tossed their cigarette butts on the forest floor, extinguished them, then turned to leave.

Matt watched as they turned on their flashlights, exited the clearing, and made their way back through the forest to their trucks. The sound of engines turning over was followed by the grating of tires over loose gravel. A moment later they were gone.

"Kyla," Matt asked. "You okay?"

No response.

"Kyla," Matt repeated, a note of urgency in his voice. "Situation report."

Kyla answered. "Give me a second," she said.

"You good?"

"Other than picking shards of glass off my neck? Just wonderful."

"That was close," Jules said.

"Yeah," Rigor said. "Welcome to Russia. Come for the vodka, stay for the gunfire."

Matt rose to his feet. "We're clear." He made a call, spoke with Alexander Kurien, provided him with their coordinates, ended the call, addressed his team. "Our ride's on the way. Gather your gear. Let's go."

Rigor walked with Matt across the open field. "You have no idea how much I wanted to blow that fucker's head off," he said. "That was close. Too close."

"That makes two of us," Matt replied.

"Your girl sure knows how to keep her shit together under pressure."

Matt nodded. "Kyla can handle herself as well as you or me, maybe even better."

Rigor held out his fist. "Good to know."

Matt fist-bumped it.

25

Not A Threat

THE JUNIOR AND senior Reconnaissance General Bureau operatives who had been assigned to watch the Park family household for the past week had been ordered to report to the office of the National Defence Commission's General Staff Department. No explanation had been given as to why the meeting had been called so suddenly. The men sat in the reception area, nervously awaiting the Minister's arrival.

Moments later, the elevator doors parted. Accompanied by his two bodyguards, Minster Ho Chang walked past them, entered his office, and shut the door. The bodyguards who had accompanied him turned and stood guard outside his office.

The younger operative turned to his supervisor, whispered. "What do you suppose this is about?"

His boss shrugged. "Could be anything. A situation report request, promotion, official notification that you're being reassigned to another operational arm. Your guess is as good as mine."

"Another operational arm?"

"Surveillance like we've been doing for the last week is the lowest level of responsibility within our department, which is probably why they stuck you with me."

"Stuck me with you. Thanks for that."

"Look, kid. The age difference between us is obvious. They've probably had their eyes on you for a while, waiting for the right opportunity to present itself. You're the up and comer. I'm the old guy with bad knees and gout in one toe. I've been doing this job for a long time, maybe too long. My job was to teach you as much as I could before the day came for me to pack it in. Officially, that's one month from today. If I had to guess, this is the day our time together comes to an end, and you receive your first permanent assignment. If you're lucky, they'll assign you to the Cyber Warfare Guidance Bureau. That's where the real action is these days. But you're also young and in great shape, so they might assign you to Special Operations or Military Intelligence. Any way that it goes, you've got a great career ahead of you. Just keep your head down and do whatever job they assign you to the best of your ability. Who knows? Maybe one day you'll be sitting behind the Minister's desk and running the show."

The young operative shook his head. "I'm not much for desk work or politics. I was built for the field, not the office."

His supervisor chuckled. "That's what you say right now. Believe me, twenty years from now, when your body starts to hurt from everything you've put it through in the field, the thought of spending your remaining days tapping away at a keyboard behind a desk starts to look really good."

The telephone on the receptionist's desk rang. She picked up the handset, listened, returned it to the cradle, spoke to the operatives. "The Minister will see you now. Please, enter."

The bodyguards stopped the men before they entered the office, motioned to them. "Arms."

The men raised their arms, waited to be patted down. The second bodyguard stood at the door, watching his partner as he conducted the pat down; first their arms, then their legs, back, and chest, his hand firmly gripping the pistol holstered at his side.

His partner stood. "Clear," he announced.

The second bodyguard removed his hand from his gun, opened the office door.

The operatives entered the room.

Minister Chang remained focused on the report he was reviewing. He pointed to the two chairs in front of his desk. "Take a seat," he said.

The men sat and waited for the minister to speak. He closed the folder, looked up. "This is all you have on Dr. Soo Park?"

The junior operative was about to speak. His superior raised his hand, quieted him, addressed the head of the Reconnaissance General Bureau. "With respect, Minister," he replied, "there's nothing to report. We've been watching the residence for two weeks now. We've noticed nothing out of the ordinary, nor have we observed any activity that would suggest Dr. Park has been in contact with her brother."

The minister tapped the file folder with his finger. "Your

report states that a deep sweep surveillance was authorized. How deep?"

The senior operative nodded. "All devices belonging to Dr. Park and her family have been monitored: cell phones, laptops... even her son's video game chat rooms. A covert listening device was planted in the home as well. We turned up nothing."

Chang leaned back in his chair, crossed his arms. "What are your thoughts on the matter? Do you feel further surveillance is needed?"

"No, sir. I do not. If Dr. Park or a member of her family had been in contact with her brother, I believe we would have discovered evidence of that by now. We haven't."

"Final thoughts?"

"Dr. Park and her family are not a threat to national security. The file should be closed. Doing so would permit us to turn our attention to more important matters."

The minister leaned forward. "Very well. We'll put a pin in her surveillance for now, but I'm not ready to close this file just yet. I want both of you to shadow her for the next two days."

"Shadow her, sir?"

"There's a conference taking place tomorrow in Vladivostok. Dr. Park and her research partner, Dr. Jin Cho, are the keynote presenters. At the behest of the Supreme Leader, the Park family has been granted the opportunity to accompany her on the trip. The information Dr's Park and Cho will be presenting is top secret. Only a handful of their scientific peers will be in attendance, together with military leaders from both the Soviet Union and North Korea. I'm assigning you to watch over Dr. Park and her family and keep them safe while they are in Russia."

"Just the Park's, sir? Not Dr. Cho as well?"

The minister shook his head. "This office has been monitoring the progress being made by Nest 5 on the project to which the doctors have been assigned. It has become clear that Dr. Park has been primarily responsible for the breakthroughs which have been made in that lab. Dr. Cho's contribution has been secondary, mostly one of validating Dr. Park's findings. Which makes Dr. Park the more valuable asset to both the RGB and the State."

The senior operative nodded. "Understood, sir."

"Your itinerary has been prepared for you. Pick it up when you leave my office. You'll be leaving immediately. Upon your arrival in Vladivostok, you are to conduct a security sweep of the conference room and all additional rooms on the floor where the presentation will take place. After you have completed your check, the floor is to be locked down and remain closed to all but the delegates themselves, Russian and North Korean security personnel, and vetted staff until the presentation has concluded. After the conference you will escort the Park's from the hotel to the border and back to their home. Do you understand the details of this assignment as I've explained them to you?"

The men nodded. "Yes, sir," the junior operative replied.

"Good." The minister turned his attention to the younger man. "Son, I would be remiss if I didn't inform you that this might be the most important assignment of your career. The eyes of this office will be on you. I suggest you impress me."

"I will, sir," the younger operative replied.

The minister nodded, returned his attention to his computer. "That will be all."

The men rose from their chairs, took their leave,

retrieved their itineraries from the front desk, rode the elevator down to the main floor.

As they walked through the lobby, the senior operative turned to his protégé. "Do you realize what just happened up there?"

The young man shook his head. "Not really."

"You just got fast tracked by the man himself. As someone who's been carrying RGB credentials for a long time, let me offer you a solid piece of career advice."

"What's that, sir?"

"Don't fuck this up."

26

Ahead Of Schedule

"HOW FAR UNTIL we rendezvous with Cross's contact?" Rigor asked.

Matt checked his phone. "The pin he dropped puts us four miles out," he replied. "We can be there in an hour if we push it."

Rigor scoffed. "Push it... over *this* terrain?" He followed Matt around a boulder. "Good luck with that. These are ankle-breaking conditions, my friend."

"Then I suggest you watch where you're walking," Matt replied.

"Thanks for the tip."

"You have to admit one thing," Kyla said as she rounded the boulder behind Jules. "It is a rather beautiful area."

"It is," Jules replied. "What the Livandyskay mountain

region lacks in hospitable terrain it makes up for in picturesque scenery."

In the pre-dawn fog, massive rocks and boulders jutted out of the ground around them like silhouetted stone sentries protecting the rugged mountainside. As their angle of descent grew less severe, the topography of the mountain changed. Ancient boulders gave way to smaller rocks, finally to a moss-covered forest floor and fast-running streams. In the distance, Matt heard the sound of a waterfall. He raised his fist, stopped. The team followed his lead.

"What's up?" Rigor asked.

Matt addressed his team. "We're two mics out. The noise of that waterfall is a problem. Keep an eye out and stay alert. The forest ahead is thick with trees, which will obstruct our sight line. We don't know how many patrols are in this region or where they're stationed. Just because we can't hear them doesn't mean they can't see us. The last thing we need is to walk right into a firefight. Copy?"

The team replied. "Copy."

Matt removed his phone, called Alexander Kurien.

"Kurien."

"It's Reaper," Matt replied. "We'll be at the location in twenty minutes. How far away are you?"

"About the same," Kurien replied.

"We're approaching the waterfall," Matt said.

"That means you're close."

"Anything I should know?"

"Yes," Kurien said. "There's a stone path at the base of the waterfall. Hikers take it to get from the mountain road to the top of the mountain. Take it. There's a massive thicket beside the road. Take cover in there and watch for me. I'll flash my high beams twice when I arrive."

"Have you noticed anything out of the ordinary?" Matt asked.

"Such as?"

"Increased ground patrols? Checkpoints? Heightened security in the area?"

"No. Why would I?"

"An increased military presence could be a sign that we were sighted when we parachuted in."

"I don't think so," Kurien replied. "Had that been the case, the mountain would be swarming with troops by now, not to mention air support looking for your team's heat signature on the ground. My drive to you has been uneventful thus far. I don't think you have anything to worry about."

"Good," Matt said. "We'll get to the waterfall and follow the path to the thicket as you instructed. See you in twenty."

"If I run into a problem, I'll call."

"Copy that."

Matt ended the call, turned to his team. "We're good. We catch our ride in twenty. Let's move."

The team followed Matt across the mossy, dew-laden terrain, over the top of the waterfall, and down the mountainside. At last, they reached the stone path.

Matt located the dense thicket Kurien had referred to, entered it, looked out. It was nearly impossible to see the road from where he stood. The brushwood and overgrowth provided excellent cover.

"This is it," Matt said. "Drop your gear and take five. Kurien will be here soon."

"Copy that," Jules said.

"Ditto," Kyla added.

Rigor checked his watch. "We're ahead of schedule," he said.

Matt nodded. "It was a long hike down the mountain. A rest will help."

"What kind of vehicle is Kurien driving?"

"A Lincoln Navigator. Why?"

Rigor parted the thicket's branches so that he could better see the road. "You hear that?" he said.

"Yeah," Matt replied. "That's him. So much for our break."

Rigor shook his head. "Not so fast, boss." He raised his weapon, held it close to his chest.

"What's up, Rig?" Matt asked.

"Whatever's coming our way, it isn't a Navigator."

Matt looked through the thicket, watched as a vehicle rounded a turn in the distance. Its engine whined as it fought the steep incline of the mountain road, then sped up when it reached level ground. It was moving fast, heading to their position.

Military.

"How the fuck did Kurien not see that vehicle?" Rigor said. "If he's a few minutes out like he said he was, it would have been ahead of him, not behind."

Matt shook his head. "I don't know."

"You think he sold us out?"

"No, I don't."

"Well, I've got news for you, bud. I'll bet you my dive business that's exactly what he did. Those assholes are here for us."

Matt sighed. "I hope you're wrong."

Rigor nodded. "Me, too. But I'm telling you, I'm not."

Matt spoke to Kyla and Jules. "If we're noticed in here,

this thicket will become a kill box. You two take overwatch. Go high and secure a vantage point. Rigor and I will stay here. If something pops off, take care of it."

"Copy that," Jules said. She hurried out of the thicket, made her way up the hill to an elevated position behind a tree twenty yards above their position. Kyla followed her, took cover between two large boulders.

The military truck rounded the corner, slowed, stopped in front of the thicket.

Matt and Rigor trained their weapons on the driver and passenger.

They waited.

27

Mom's Famous!

AS THE RECONNAISSANCE General Bureau's convoy reached the Russian border and waited for their passports and security documents to be cleared by the border soldiers, Tam squeezed his mother's hand as he looked out the window. "Wow," he said. "Is this it, Mom? Are we really in Russia?"

Soo nodded. "Yes, we are."

Tam took in the commotion which came with their arrival. "Geez, Mom," he said. "You must be really important."

Soo laughed. "What makes you say that?"

Tam pointed to the lineup of Russian police cars, marked and unmarked, positioned in front of the RGB convoy, their service lights flashing. "We're getting a police escort!"

Soo glanced out the window. "We are."

Tam turned around in his chair, spoke to his grandmother seated directly behind him. "Check it out, Gran," he said. "Mom's famous!"

"I'm sure that welcome is being extended to all of us, grandson, not just your mother," Gran replied.

Minho was not as impressed by the pomp and circumstance happening outside as was his master. He lay on the floor of the bus, lifted his head momentarily when he heard Tam's voice, sniffed the air, then yawned and went back to sleep.

The bus door opened. A Russian guard boarded the vehicle, sharply dressed in a green camouflage uniform, large green hat, and white gloves. A red sash crossed his chest above his yellow belt. He addressed the passengers. "Good morning, ladies and gentlemen," he said. "I trust your journey has been pleasant so far?"

Soo and her colleagues nodded, expressed their agreement.

"Excellent," he continued. "Welcome to the Border Service of the Federal Security Service of the Russian Federation. You have reached the official border between our two great nations. On behalf of our president, may I express what an honor it is to have such a distinguished delegation visit our country. As you may have noticed, we have assembled a security detail to escort you to your hotel in Vladivostok. While in Russia, we kindly ask that you familiarize yourselves with our laws and customs and obey them at all times during your visit. We will do everything within our power to ensure that your visit will be an enjoyable and memorable experience. Please bear with us for a few minutes while we process your papers." The guard touched the brim of his wide hat and smiled. "Have a wonderful conference," he said, then departed the bus.

Tam was all smiles. "Wow!" he said. "Did you see how he was dressed, Mom? Too cool!"

Soo smiled. "Yes. He looked very sharp indeed."

Gran spoke. "If you're this excited just crossing the border, I can't imagine what you'll be like when you see the hotel."

"I know, right?" Tam replied. "Waaay cool!"

Jin sat across the aisle from Soo. "It is exciting, isn't it?" she said.

Soo glanced at her, nodded. Her demeanor was cool. "It is."

"We'll have to get together when we arrive at the hotel," Jin continued. "We should go over our notes one more time before we present tomorrow."

"Why?" Soo asked. "Are you not prepared?"

"Of course. It's just that—"

"Then I see no reason for us to meet."

Jin knew why Soo was being short with her. She had told her that she had found the listening device that had been hidden in the dog's toy. "Soo, you need to let me explain."

Soo leaned across the aisle, whispered her response. "Stay away from me and my family, Dr. Cho. Don't make me tell you again."

Jin sat back in her seat, closed her eyes. The RGB was to blame for Soo's loss of trust in her. She had done nothing wrong. Never would she have agreed to spy on her colleague and someone she considered a friend. The planting of the listening device was a situation not of her making. It had been forced upon her. She understood Soo's anger and apprehension. When the time was right they would talk, and she would tell her about the events that had transpired at the shopping center and how the RGB had snatched her off the street, taken her to a secret location, and forced her to participate in the surveillance of the family.

The bus shuddered. Its sudden movement pulled her out of the unpleasant memory.

Ahead, the vehicles in the police escort turned on their sirens.

Slowly, they crossed the border into Russia.

28

A Little Problem

THE SOLDIERS EXITED their vehicle, stretched, conversed. One man motioned to the other, pointed to the forest. His friend laughed, removed a package of cigarettes from his jacket pocket, lit up a smoke, leaned against the truck's grill, took in the remarkable view of the rugged mountainside that lay before him. Cirrus clouds of hammered purple and blood orange gave the Livandyskay's a majestic appearance. The man took a deep draw on his cigarette, called out to his fellow soldier.

The team heard Jules's voice in their earbuds. She interpreted the conversation.

"Our man is relieving himself," she whispered. "His buddy is telling him to hurry up."

The soldier flicked away his cigarette, retrieved a bottle of water from the cab of the truck, took a long swig, tossed the bottle back into the cab, walked along the road, took in the view. He called out again.

Jules updated the team. "He's asking him what's taking so long." Jules waited for the second man to reply. "He's joking, says he has a weak bladder."

She watched through her rifle scope as he zipped up his fly, stepped out from behind the bushes, and made his way out of the heavy brush back to the truck and rejoined his partner. After the two spoke briefly, the second man wandered off.

"Apparently, our rendezvous point is also a pee stop for Russian forces," Kyla said. "Guy number two is sniffing out a place to take care of business."

"Hold your position," Matt whispered. "Don't spook them. They'll be on their way in a minute."

"Hopefully so will we," Rigor said.

Matt nodded.

Having relieved himself, the second man walked down the mountainside, called out to his friend, pointed.

From a distance came the sound of an approaching vehicle.

"You hear that?" Matt asked.

"Yeah," Rigor replied. "Must be Kurien."

"Kyla, Jules," Matt said. "Either of you have eyes on that vehicle?"

Kyla shifted her rifle scope to the left, searched the mountain road, found the car, replied. "Affirmative. It's an SUV. Black. Lincoln Navigator."

Jules watched as the men opened the truck doors, withdrew their assault rifles, then stood beside one another in the middle of the road. "Looks like the tinkle twins plan to stop the SUV," she said. "Probably want to ask the driver what he's doing up here at this hour of the morning."

"Kurien said his Nav has diplomatic plates," Matt answered. "He's not required to answer their questions."

"Yeah, but we're up in the mountains," Rigor said. "Who knows? Maybe these guys aren't going anywhere. Maybe they're here to block the road. Could be there's a field training exercise taking place near here. If that's the case, diplomatic tags or not, they'll order him to turn around and leave."

Kyla shifted her position behind the boulder. Frightened by the sudden movement below, a flock of birds perched high in the trees above her cackled loudly, then took to the sky.

One of the soldiers turned around. He watched the birds fly away, then walked toward the stone path.

"Shit," Kyla said.

"What is it?" Matt whispered.

"The birds got tinkler number two's attention."

The team watched as the soldier raised his rifle, peered through his scope, surveyed the woods and the surrounding treetops.

"He's curious," Rigor said.

The soldier reached the path, called out to his partner.

"He said he's going to check out what spooked the birds out of the treetop," Jules reported. "He told his partner to stop the car and that he'll be back in a minute."

"I don't like this, Matt," Rigor whispered. "Not one bit."

The soldier stepped beyond the tree line, entered the edge of the forest.

Kyla and Jules dropped low, stayed hidden, listened as dry leaves and fallen branches crunched and snapped beneath the weight of the man's footfalls as he walked up the mountainside and stopped twenty feet from their position.

Jules stole a glance at the soldier, watched as he stood beneath the massive tree which had been the birds' resting place, looked up, then briefly investigated the surrounding area. Satisfied that no threat existed, he turned, walked back down the path, then froze in his tracks.

Kyla followed him with her scope, watched as a flash of light suddenly emanated from inside the thicket.

"Matt, Rigor... don't move," she whispered.

Matt lay on the ground inside the thick bramble, his rifle aimed at the soldier.

The soldier raised his weapon, pointed it towards the thicket, called out to his partner.

"He's telling him to forget the car and to cover him," Jules said. "I think you're burned, Matt."

Matt issued the command. "Execute."

Thwup.

Thwup.

The sound-suppressed rounds from Kyla and Jules's weapons found their targets.

The headshots dropped the two soldiers to the ground, dead.

Jules and Kyla broke from cover, hurried down the mountainside, rejoined Matt and Rigor as they emerged from their hiding place inside the thicket.

"How the hell did he see us?" Rigor asked.

Jules touched the altimeter on Rigor's wrist. "He didn't see you. He saw that. The sun came up and peeked through the clouds. When it did, it hit the glass face of your altimeter. The flash of light caught his attention."

"We need to move fast," Matt said. "Rig, on me. We'll retrieve the body from the road and hide the truck. Jules and Kyla, deal with this guy. Drag him into the thicket and cover him with branches."

"Copy that," Kyla said.

The women carried out Matt's orders.

Matt and Rigor hurried down to the road. Matt dragged the dead soldier's body to the rear of the vehicle and tossed him into the truck bed as Rigor jumped behind the wheel and started the vehicle.

"Think this thing can handle off-road terrain?" Matt asked.

Rigor nodded. "Piece of cake."

"Good," Matt said. "Get rid of it."

Rigor dropped the truck into gear, drove it up the steep mountainside until he reached the stone path, then drove the vehicle into the woods. When he was satisfied that the truck could not be seen from the road, he shut off the vehicle, jumped out of the cab, and ran down the stone path to meet up with Matt, Kyla, and Jules.

The Lincoln Navigator rounded the corner, came to a stop. Alexander Kurien opened his door, stepped out of the vehicle, addressed Matt. "Reaper?" he asked.

Matt nodded. "You're late," he replied.

"My apologies," Kurien replied. "I ran into a problem."

"Problem?"

Kurien nodded. "The Federal police are setting up road-blocks going into and out of Vladivostok."

"You think they're looking for us?" Kyla asked.

Kurien shook his head. "If the police or military were actively searching for you, they'd have shut down every mountain access road. I don't think you have anything to fear. As I said, my diplomatic plates will get us anywhere we need to go. We won't be stopped."

"We ran into a little problem of our own," Matt said.

"How so?"

"We drew the attention of a couple of soldiers."

"And?"

Matt turned and pointed. "One body is in the thicket. The second is in a truck parked in the forest."

Kurien nodded. "That is most definitely a problem. Don't worry. I'll make a call. My people will take care of it."

"Thank you," Matt replied.

"The troops that patrol this area are required to check in every hour," Kurien said. "Gather your gear and change your clothes. We need to leave. Now."

Matt nodded. "Copy that."

29

_____

Contact

TAM STARED OUT the window, watching as the phalanx of Russian police cars escorted the convoy from the Russian border to Vladivostok. He turned to his mother, a broad smile on his face. "Man, talk about getting the VIP treatment!"

Soo nodded. "They're certainly making a great impression."

"I'll say!" Tam replied. He looked down as a motorcycle policeman matched the bus's speed. Tam waved. To his amusement, the officer looked up, smiled, waved back, toggled his siren on and off, then sped ahead up the road.

Gran leaned forward. She spoke to Soo between the seats. "That boy is not going to sleep a wink tonight. I've never seen him this excited before."

Soo smiled. "I know. You have to admit it, though. It is quite a spectacle."

"Do you think the president will be there, Mom?" Tam asked.

Soo shook her head. "I doubt that very much, son."

Tam looked disappointed. "But it's possible, right?"

Soo nodded. "Of course. Anything is possible. But the president has a whole country to run. I'm quite sure attending our little conference isn't at the top of his priority list."

Twenty minutes after leaving the border, the convoy entered the city of Vladivostok.

Tam stared up at the office towers lining the main road as they drove through the downtown core. At last, the bus came to a stop. The police cars and motorcycles turned off their sirens but left their red and blue service lights flashing.

The bus driver called out. "We're here, folks. Welcome to the Grand Hotel Vladivostok. Please collect your belongings and disembark from the bus in single file. Suitcases and travel cases will be offloaded by the porters shortly. The hotel's event coordinator is waiting for you. Please gather in the lobby and await further instructions. Have a great conference."

The bus driver's announcement was met with a round of applause.

Tam shot up out of his seat, shuffled past his mother, and tugged on Minho's leash. The dog had been sleeping peacefully for the duration of the trip. He rose to his feet, stretched, and wagged his tail. "Come on, boy," Tam said excitedly. "Let's check it out!"

"Make sure Minho does his business first," Soo said as

she retrieved her computer bag from the storage compartment above her seat.

"Sure thing, Mom," Tam replied. He addressed Minho. "You heard Mom. No peeing or pooping in the hotel. Let's go, Furface."

Minho chuffed, pulled Tam behind him as he jumped down from the bus, then made his way straight to the nearest tree and relieved himself.

"Good boy," Tam said.

Mother and grandmother waited as the porters removed the two small hard-shell rolling suitcases Gran had packed for the trip. Soo turned to her mother. "When you said you packed light you really meant it!"

"You said we'd only be away for a couple of days," Gran replied. "I packed the essentials, plus a smart-looking suit for you to wear for your presentation."

"I'm kidding, Mom," Soo replied. "I'm sure you've got all the bases covered."

Tam piped up. "Did you pack my Nintendo, Gran?" he asked.

"Yes, Tam," Gran replied. "I packed your Nintendo."

"What about treats for Minho?"

"Yes, grandson. Minho has enough treats to last him for the next two days."

"Which kind?"

"Excuse me?"

"Minho prefers crunchy biscuits over chewy snacks."

"I know. I packed his crunchy biscuits."

"And his vitamins?"

"Yes."

"Brush and comb?"

"Of course."

"Mr. Raccoon?"

Gran paused. She looked at Soo. "No, I didn't pack Mr. Raccoon. You decapitated him when you two were rough-housing. Remember?"

"Sure," Tam replied. "But head or no head, he still loves Mr. Raccoon."

Soo walked over to her son. "Listen, Tam," she said. "About what you found when Mr. Raccoon's head got pulled off."

"Yeah?"

"I need you to keep that a secret. Don't mention it to anybody, especially while you're here. Do you understand?"

Tam shrugged. "I guess so."

Soo spoke sternly. "I'm serious, Tam. I can't explain to you why it's so important that you don't talk about it right now, especially while we're here, but I will when we get home. I promise."

Tam nodded. "Sure, Mom. No problem."

Soo tousled her son's hair playfully. "That's my boy."

Minho whined as a police officer passed him, accompanied by his K-9 partner. The dog sniffed the luggage on the porters' cart, then entered the building as the automatic doors parted.

"Sorry, buddy," Tam said. "That's a police dog, and he's working. He doesn't have time to play with you."

Minho panted, clearly excited to see another dog at the hotel.

"Excuse me, Dr. Soo Park?"

Soo turned around. "Yes?"

A man stood before her. His face bore a pleasant smile. He extended his hand. "My name is Dr. Kyu-Ho Kim. We haven't yet had the pleasure of meeting."

Soo smiled. "Very nice to meet you, Dr. Kim. Please allow me to introduce my family. This is my mother, my son, Tam, and our dog, Minho."

Dr. Kim bowed respectfully. "It's my honor."

"Are you presenting at the conference, Dr. Kim?" Soo asked.

Dr. Kim shook his head. "No. I'm here in a strictly 'observe and report' capacity."

"Observe and report?"

"For our Supreme Leader," Dr. Kim replied. He leaned in, whispered. "I'll be awarding the National Medal of Distinction at the conclusion of this event. My job is to rate each presentation and determine a winner. I've been provided with information on all Nest 5 researchers. I was told that your research, and that of your colleague, Dr. Cho, represents a significant breakthrough in the field of chemical and biological warfare."

Soo nodded. "We believe it does."

"Then I'll be looking forward to evaluating your presentation," Kim replied. "Well, I won't take up any more of your time. I see your fellow delegates are checking in. I'm sure you're eager to do the same. Perhaps we'll have an opportunity to talk again later?"

Soo smiled. "I hope so."

"Very good," Kim said. "Enjoy your day."

"Thank you, Dr. Kim," Soo replied. "We will."

Gran watched the young doctor walk away. She nudged her daughter playfully. "See that?" she said.

"See what?" Soo asked.

"His butt. Nice. Very nice."

"Mom!"

"What? I may be old, but I still know a great butt when I see one."

Soo shook her head. "You're incorrigible, you know that?"

Gran smiled. "Did you notice he wasn't wearing a ring?"

"Mom, cut it out. I'm here to work, nothing more."

"Make sure you get his number before you leave."

Soo rolled her eyes. "Oh, brother. Come on. Let's check in. It was an early start to the day and I'm tired. I could use a quick nap."

"No problem," Gran replied. "When you check us in, make sure you ask the desk clerk for Dr. Hottie's room number."

"Dr. Hottie?"

"Hey, if you're not going to take a shot, I will."

Soo laughed. "You're impossible." She called out to Tam, who was checking out a floral display on a massive granite table in the middle of the lobby. "Come on, buddy," she said. "Time to check in."

Kim watched from across the lobby as Soo and her family engaged in a friendly exchange with the front desk clerk, accepted their room card keys and welcome package, then headed toward the elevators with Minho. He removed his cell phone and made a call.

"Yes?"

"It's me," he said. "I've made contact."

30

Best Before Date

MATT AND HIS team slipped out of their parachuting jumpsuits. The travel clothes they wore beneath the garment... jeans, casual shirt, lightweight jacket, nylon backpack, and running shoes... would be suitable attire to wear for their check-in at the Grand Vladivostok. They stowed their weapons and gear in the rear compartment of the Navigator.

"Diplomatic plates or not," Rigor said as he settled into the backseat of the Navigator beside Jules, "I can't say I like the feeling of being unarmed knowing that we'll be crossing through Russian security checkpoints in the next few minutes."

"That makes two of us," Jules said.

"Make that three," Kyla agreed.

"Forget it," Matt said. "Alexander knows what he's doing.

We're attending a conference, remember? How many other attendees do you figure will be carrying?"

Rigor sighed. "None."

"Precisely."

"You have nothing to worry about, my friends," Kurien said. "There isn't an FSB agent or police officer who would dare stop this vehicle. When they run the plate at the checkpoint, which they will, it will come back as assigned to the president's motorcade. All they are permitted to do is mirror check the underside of the car for possible security threats. That's it."

"You mean conduct an explosives sweep," Matt said.

"Correct," Kurien replied. "And we are not required to exit the vehicle in order for them to do that."

Matt nodded. "Must be nice to have friends in high places."

Kurien smiled. "Here in Russia those are the only friends to have."

"How long were you with the agency?" Matt asked.

"Twenty years," Kurien replied. "That was long enough. I was already beginning to feel like I'd reached my best before date. It was time to get out. I preferred to make the decision to retire before someone did it for me... permanently, if you know what I mean."

"I do," Matt agreed.

"The day after I left the agency I got an offer to provide personal protection for a visiting dignitary. I wasn't necessarily interested in the job, but the compensation was too generous to turn down. My client's government paid me more for that weekend of work than the CIA had paid me for an entire year. Unfortunately, there was a problem. We came under fire outside of Moscow while returning to his hotel. I could tell by the way the driver handled the car that the men who attacked us were professionals. Despite my best efforts I couldn't shake them. I dropped my window the second I had the chance, pulled a one-eighty, locked up the brakes, and unloaded my MAC-10 into our pursuers as they passed by. I watched their car roll several times before exploding. No one got out, so there was no need for me to finish them off. The fire took care of that. I got my client out of there and returned him to his hotel, safe and sound. He insisted on paying me a bonus for saving his life. I told him it wasn't necessary, that it was part of the job, but he wouldn't hear of it. Before I knew it, my phone was blowing up. Not only had he referred all his friends to me, but he insisted that I start a company and that he would finance everything. He wouldn't accept no for an answer and, quite frankly, I liked the idea. The personal protection agency we started is now the largest in Russia."

Matt smiled. "I'll bet you're glad you took that call."

Kurien nodded. "I am. It changed my life."

The Navigator rounded a blind corner. Ahead, a line of cars waited to be processed through a police checkpoint.

"They were setting this up while I was coming to pick you up," Kurien said. He reminded the team: "Remember what I said. We'll be through this in a minute. Stay calm."

"Copy that," Matt replied.

The Navigator approached the checkpoint.

A young officer motioned for Kurien to lower his window. He refused to comply.

The officer banged his fist against the window and repeated his command.

No response from inside the Navigator.

Angry that the driver was ignoring him, the officer

raised his weapon and barked the order for what he said would be the last time.

Kurien turned on the Nav's red and blue service lights, opened its external communications system, and yelled his response at the officer.

The policeman immediately stepped away from the vehicle and permitted them to pass through the checkpoint.

Jules laughed. "Someone got the message loud and clear."

"What did you say?" Rigor asked.

Kurien answered. "I reminded him that this is a diplomatic vehicle, that he was a fucking idiot for not recognizing the car and its plates, and that if he didn't let us pass I'd see to it that he spends the rest of his career as a school crossing guard."

Rigor smiled. "Nice one."

Kurien nodded. "I thought so."

"How far are we from Vladivostok?" Matt asked.

"Thirty minutes."

"We'll need access to our weapons and gear when we get there."

"That won't be a problem," Kurien replied. "The Grand has special VIP travel cases which they make available for visiting dignitaries and diplomats. You'll transfer your gear into them. I have a roll of embossed tape in the glove compartment which bears the seal of the Russian consulate. Once I apply that tape to the case it is considered the property of the Russian government. No one but me is permitted to open it."

"Is the tape legit?" Matt asked.

Kurien glanced at him. "Maybe it is, maybe it isn't."

Matt smiled. "You've covered all the bases, haven't you?"

Kurien shrugged. "In our line of work one can never be too prepared."

"Falcon told me you'd be a valuable asset for us," Matt replied. "I'll make sure he knows just how much you came through."

"If it's all the same to you, Reaper, I suggest we hold off on the accolades until your mission has been completed."

"Fair enough," Matt replied.

In the distance, an immense tower rose above its neighboring buildings in the city's downtown core.

"There it is," Kurien said. "The Grand Vladivostok Hotel."

Minutes later, the Navigator entered the Grand's underground parking lot. Kurien waited for the electronic scanner mounted on the VIP ONLY parking gate to read the bar code on the diplomatic plate.

The code was accepted. The gate rose.

"We're in," Kurien said.

31

Not A Vacation

T AM CALLED OUT. "Wow! Check out the view! It
goes on forever!"

Soo walked to her tenth-floor hotel window,
joined her son, and looked out. In the distance, dozens of
ocean-faring cargo vessels occupied the docks of the Port of
Vladivostok. Massive cranes positioned atop drivable plat-
forms inched along the dock, then stopped, extended their
robotic arms, and began loading and unloading steel shipping containers from the ships.

"Impressive, isn't it?" Soo asked.

"It's more than impressive," Tam stated. "It's awesome!"
The boy looked up at his mother. "Can Minho and I go
check out the hotel and the dock?"

"By yourself?" Soo said. "Absolutely not!"

"But Mom!"

"No buts, Tam. We're in a foreign country. You can't just go gallivanting about unsupervised."

Tam turned to his grandmother. "Gran, you want to go to the docks to see the ships?"

"Nice try, kiddo," Soo said. "Don't even think about pulling the grandmother card on me. I'm the one who says where we go and what we do while we're here, not gran."

"But you said you wanted to lie down and have a nap," Tam reminded her. "What are Minho and I supposed to do for the next hour?"

Soo knew the boy was much too excited to sit quietly while she slept, which means she wouldn't get a second's rest. "Tell you what. We'll spend an hour looking around, but not at the docks. Gran isn't up for that long of a walk and neither am I. There's plenty to see in the hotel and the surrounding shops. Does that sound like a fair compromise?"

"Can we go to the docks later?" Tam pleaded. "Please?"

Soo nodded. "If we have time. Remember, this is a business trip, not a vacation. There are people here whom I report to. They'll tell us how much free time we'll be given. I'm sure they'll arrange a tour for us. Maybe a visit to the docks will be part of that tour."

Tam sighed. "Sorry, Mom. You're right. I forgot this was a business trip."

"And it's not just important for me. You have a presentation to deliver, too."

Tam shrugged. "That's no big deal. I can do mine with my eyes closed."

Soo smiled. "Is that so?"

Tam nodded. "Yup."

"Okay, Mr. Brainiac. What do you plan to talk about?"

"I'm not sure yet."

"Not sure? You present tomorrow!"

"I'm still trying to decide between two topics."

"Just pick one and go with it."

"It's not that simple."

"Why not?"

"I don't know how smart these people are," Tam explained. "The subject matter might be above them. They might not get it."

Soo suppressed a smile. "Is that so?"

Tam nodded.

"Honey, the people attending this conference are among the smartest minds in both North Korea and Russia," Soo said. "I'm sure they'll be able to understand anything you talk about."

"Maybe," Tam replied.

"What topics are you considering?"

"Either what the long-term effects of artificial intelligence might be on the development of future surgical innovations, or how digital literacy will influence human capital as it applies to increased global mobility. Which one do you think they'd rather hear about?"

Soo stared at her son, lost for words. "A.I. is a pretty hot topic these days. I'd go with number one."

Tam shrugged. "Okay."

"Make sure you review your notes first. You don't want to forget anything."

"Notes?"

Soo nodded. "You have notes, right?"

Tam shook his head. "Nah."

"Why not?"

"Don't need 'em." Tam raised a finger to his head, tapped

it. "I have an eidetic memory, remember? Once I learn something I never forget it. And both subjects are a piece of cake."

Soo smiled. "You're a pretty special kid, you know that?"

"That's what everybody keeps telling me," Tam replied.

Soo checked her appearance in the mirror, touched up her hair. "All right," she said. "What do you say we check out this place while we have the time?"

"Yes!" Tam yelled. He attached Minho's leash to his collar. "Come on, boy. Let's go!"

Minho stood, chuffed, waved his tail excitedly, and accompanied his master to the hotel door.

"All set, Mom?" Soo asked her mother.

Gran shook her head. "You two go on without me. These old joints are tired. I think I'll lie down until you get back."

"You sure?"

Gran nodded as she turned down the bedsheets. "Have fun. Tam, listen to your mother. Don't wander off. You hear me?"

Tam stepped into the hallway with Minho. "I won't, Gran."

"Promise?"

"Promise."

"Good boy."

Soo helped her mother into bed, pulled her blankets up to her neck, tucked her in, kissed her forehead. "Get some rest, Mom. We'll see you soon."

"Have fun," Gran replied.

"We will."

"Do me a favor, dear?"

"Sure. What's that?"

Gran smiled. "Get me that nice Dr. Kim's phone number."

Soo shook her head and laughed. "Go to sleep."

Tam, Soo, and Minho rode the elevator down to the ground floor. When the doors opened, they walked through the lobby and out the front door.

Unlike the traditionally cold weather for which Vladivostok was well known, this morning had brought with it the warmth of the sun. A comfortable breeze greeted them as they left the hotel and walked along the sidewalk, observing the shops.

Across the street, the two operatives who had been surveilling Soo and the Park family crossed the road and fell in step half a block behind them.

32

VIP

TOGETHER WITH KURIEN, Matt and his team exited the Navigator. The reserved VIP lot was located on the second parking level of the Grand Vladivostok Hotel.

"Leave everything in the vehicle for the moment," Kurien said. "I'll pick up the key cards to the Presidential Suite from the front desk." He pointed across the lot. "That elevator is private. It offers direct access from the parking garage to floors nineteen and twenty, the top two floors. We're on twenty. Nineteen is in use. I don't know by whom, but I'll find out."

"Why is it important you know who is on that floor?" Jules asked.

Kurien smiled. "In my business, where diplomats and dignitaries rely on me for their personal protection, it's crucial that I stay one step ahead of the threat. It's what I don't know that concerns me the most."

"Copy that," Jules replied.

"I'll come with you," Matt said.

Kurien nodded. "As you wish."

Matt addressed his team. "It would be best if everyone stayed in the Nav and out of sight until we get back."

"I agree," Kurien added.

"You've got it, boss," Rigor said. He hopped back into the vehicle, closed the door. Jules and Kyla followed suit.

Matt and Kurien exited the elevator, entered the lobby, and walked to the front desk. The clerk greeted Kurien immediately.

"Mr. Kurien," he said. "So nice to see you again. Thank you for once again choosing the Grand Vladivostok for your business needs. How can I help you this morning?"

"The Presidential Suite has been reserved in my name," Kurien replied. "I'll need five key cards, please."

"Of course, sir," the clerk replied. "Give me one moment to activate them for you."

Kurien and Matt observed the activity in the lobby. "You're quite busy this morning," Kurien commented.

The clerk looked up from his computer as he passed each electronic key card through a reading device, activated them. "Yes, sir," he said. "It's a scientific conference."

Kurien feigned interest. "Is that so?"

The clerk nodded. "They've booked out all six suites on the nineteenth floor." He leaned forward, as if to share a secret. "North Koreans," he whispered. "Military, by the look of them."

Kurien nodded slowly. "Really!"

"We've never had North Koreans stay as guests in the

Grand before. To tell you the truth, we're all a little nervous."

"Nervous?" Kurien asked. "Why is that?"

"Because they're, well... North Koreans."

"I'm sure you have nothing to be concerned about," Kurien assured him. "They're just people like you and me." He winked. "If it makes you feel better, my friends and I saw no signs of invasion upon our arrival."

The clerk knew he had probably shared too much. "I'm sorry," he said. "I didn't mean to imply—"

Kurien waved his hand as the clerk passed him the activated key cards. "Don't worry about it. We are living in dangerous and uncertain times. No one can blame you for being afraid of something you don't understand."

The clerk smiled nervously. "Is there anything else I can do for you, Mr. Kurien?"

Matt interjected. "There is. Is there a clothier nearby?"

The clerk nodded. "Yes. Rostov's. It's located just around the corner from the hotel. They cater to both men and women. Very high-end apparel."

"Thank you," Matt said.

"You're welcome, sir," the clerk replied. "Enjoy your stay."

Matt and Kurien stepped away from the desk. "Well, now you know who's staying on nineteen," Matt said. "Must be the security detail for the North Korean scientists."

Kurien smiled. "Like the saying goes, keep your friends close—"

"— and your enemies even closer," Matt finished.

"Precisely. It's good to know our enemies are one floor below us."

"Personally, I'd prefer it if they were anywhere else but here," Matt said.

"Come now, Reaper," Kurien said with a smile. "Where's the fun in that?"

Matt nodded. "We need to get back to the team. Where are the cases you referred to?"

"Follow me," Kurien said.

The men entered an anteroom beside the hotel's reception desk. Four large black cases stood behind a velvet rope and stanchions in the corner of the room. The brass sign hanging from the rope read VIP USE ONLY.

"Take two cases and follow me," Kurien said.

Matt moved the stanchion aside, wheeled out two cases, and followed Kurien across the lobby to the private elevator. "I feel like a roadie for a rock band," he said.

Kurien laughed.

The VIP level elevator doors parted when they reached their parking level. Matt and Kurien wheeled the four cases over to the Navigator, unlocked them.

The team stepped out of the SUV.

"Everything good, boss?" Rigor asked.

Matt nodded. "Let's get the gear upstairs. There's a clothier located beside the hotel. It's time to look the part."

"Does this mean I'll have to wear a suit and tie?" Rigor asked as he helped transfer their weapons and gear from the Navigator into the cases.

Matt smiled. "Yes, you will."

Rigor shook his head in dismay. "Great."

"What are you complaining about?" Jules said. "You look great in a suit."

"This is true," Rigor replied. "There's no denying that I'm runway model handsome. But I don't *feel* great in a suit. We live in the Caribbean, remember? Shirt, shorts, sandals, and sunglasses. That's my kind of suit."

"Suck it up, buttercup," Jules said. "You can handle it for a day or two."

Rigor placed his MK18 assault rifle in the case. "Yeah, whatever." He closed the case and secured the latches. "Ready to roll."

"Same here," Kyla said.

Kurien opened the Nav's front passenger door, retrieved a wide roll of tape from the glove box, which bore the Russian diplomatic seal. He ran the tape across the case's openings and latches, pressed it in place. "There," he said. "We're good."

Matt rolled his case toward the elevator. "Come on," he said. "Let's get this out of the way."

"Copy that," Kyla replied.

Kurien and the team followed.

33

A Clean Getaway

TAM'S MOUTH FELL open as the family rounded the corner from the Grand hotel. The magnificent structure known as the Giavyi Universalnyi Magazin was one of the most beautiful structures he had ever seen, incorporating elements of art nouveau and baroque architecture in its design.

"Holy smoke, Mom," he exclaimed. "What is *that*?"

Soo shook her head. "I don't know."

"It's incredible, isn't it?"

Soo nodded. "It certainly is."

A woman exited the building, her arms laden with shopping bags. The logo on the bag read GUM.

"I think it's a department store," Tam said. "Can we go in, Mom? Please?"

Soo shook her head. "I don't know if we can, Tam," Soo

replied. "Not with Minho. If this store is anything like the ones back home, dogs aren't allowed inside."

"If anyone asks, I'll tell them Minho is my emotional support dog. They'll buy that."

"I can't do that, Tam."

"Why not?"

"Because it would be lying."

"Ah, come on, Mom," Tam pleaded. "The worst that'll happen is they'll kick us out. Big deal. When are we ever going to visit a Russian department store again?"

Soo smiled. "You must get your renegade attitude from your grandmother."

Tam nodded. "Yeah. Gran's a badass."

Soo acquiesced. "Okay. Just this one time. But if someone tells us that dogs aren't allowed in the store and we're asked to leave, we go. Got it?"

Tam smiled. "Got it!" The boy handed his mother Minho's leash. "Wait a sec."

Soo took the leash. "What are you doing?"

Tam opened the front door, peeked inside. "Checking for security."

"Tam Park, you get back here this inst—"

Tam waved his hand, whispered. "Okay, Mom. The guard just walked around the corner. The coast is clear. Let's go!"

Soo and Minho followed Tam into the store.

It was as beautiful on the inside as it was on the outside.

"Whoa," Tam exclaimed. "Sweet!"

Soo handed Tam Minho's leash. "Forgetting your *emotional support* dog?"

"Oh, yeah," Tam replied. "Sorry, Mom. Come on, boy. Let's check it out."

Minho plodded along beside Tam, his tail wagging lazily. Even on the days when he was most excited, the dog rarely made a sound. Where some dogs were loud, Minho was quiet, which at this moment was a very good attribute to have.

Soo and Tam wandered through the GUM's various departments and its souvenir store, checking out Russian-made designer clothes, shoes, perfumes, trinkets, and toys.

Tam was amazed. "I've never seen anything like this in my life," he said. "Have you, Mom?"

The GUM was a far cry from the basic people's supply stores in North Korea.

Soo shook her head. "No, I haven't."

"People get to live like this?" Tam exclaimed. "Incredible."

Soo could sense the emotional impact the store was having on her son. The GUM, and Russian life in general, represented a far different world from the one they were accustomed to.

"I don't understand, Mom," Tam said.

"What?"

Tam looked around the store. "How come we don't have stores like this? Ours are so... plain."

"Russia is governed much differently than our country, Tam," Soo explained. "Our Supreme Leader doesn't see the necessity for us to own such luxuries."

Tam walked to a nearby clothing rack, selected a beautiful dress, held it up, showed it to his mother. "Are you saying our Supreme Leader wouldn't think you'd look incredible in this dress?"

Soo blushed. "Thank you, Tam. That's very nice of you to say."

"He'd have to be blind not to," Tam replied, a note of anger in his voice. "Or just plain stupid."

"Tam!" Soo replied. "Don't ever say anything like that about our Supreme Leader again. Not here or back home!"

Tam returned the dress to the rack. "It's the truth. It isn't fair. If I had money, I'd buy this dress for you right now."

Soo smiled. "Thank you, sweetheart."

"Maybe we should move."

"Move?"

"Yeah. You, me, gran, and Minho. We can move here, to Russia."

Soo sighed. "I'm afraid that's something we won't be able to do."

Tam shrugged. "Why not?"

"Because it wouldn't be permitted."

"Says who?"

"Our Supreme Leader."

"Yeah? Well, screw him."

"Tam!"

Tam stared at the floor. "Sorry."

"Maybe coming to this store wasn't such a good idea after all," Soo said. "I'm sorry."

"Nah. It's okay. I guess it's just the luck of the draw, right?"

"Luck of the draw?"

"Where you're born," Tam said.

Soo placed her hand under her son's chin, raised it, stared into his eyes. "We have a good life, Tam. We might not have all this fancy stuff, but we have each other, and Gran, and Minho. I have a good job, and one day you will too. We don't want for anything. Remember the lady you saw walking out the door carrying all those bags? Just because she has the opportunity to buy those things doesn't mean that she's happy, right? At the end of the day, they're just *things*. Personally, I'll take fond memories over things any day of the week. Like this moment right now, being with the most important man in the world to me: you."

Tam shrugged. "I suppose you're right."

"Of course, I'm right. I'm your mother. I'm always right."

Tam smiled. "Yes, ma'am."

"What do you say we get out of here?" Soo asked. "We've only been in one store so far. I'm sure there are others you'd like to check out."

"Sounds like a plan."

Minho chuffed.

"Uh-oh," Tam said.

"What?"

"Security guard, nine o'clock."

Soo smiled. "We should probably get out of here before we get busted."

"Yep."

Tam, Minho, and Soo hurried out the front door just as the security guard called out after them.

Tam looked back at the chubby guard, watched him step out the door, observe them for a few seconds, then reenter the store. He laughed. "That's what I call a clean getaway! Way to go, Mom!"

Soo laughed. "We are *not* doing that again! Got it?"

"Got it."

Soo and Tam stared into the storefront window of a candy shop located several stores down the street from GUM. They watched in amazement as an elderly man dressed in confectioner's whites worked a large batch of still-warm caramel back and forth on a long quartz table, repeatedly stretching and folding the gooey mass back on top of itself, repeating the process until he was satisfied that the candy had reached its required consistency. He used a rolling pin to level out the candy, smoothing it out until it covered the entire length and width of the quartz table, then walked away, leaving the slab to cool.

"Wow!" Tam said. "Did you see that? Neat!"

Soo nodded. "He certainly has the process down to a fine art, doesn't he?"

"I'll say!"

Soo stared at her reflection in the window, which also reflected the buildings and people across the street from where they stood. Unlike the other pedestrians who paid no attention to them as they enjoyed their sightseeing day, two men stood alone. They appeared to be watching them. An uneasy feeling came over her.

"Tam, honey," she said, "you mind if we cut this walk short?"

Tam objected. "Do we have to? It was just getting good!"

"We'll see more of the city before we leave. Like I said earlier, I'm a little tired. Gran's back in the room having a nap. The lab has arranged a delegate's dinner which I'll be attending tonight. I want to be well-rested for it. Okay?"

Tam sighed. "Okay."

As they turned away from the candy shop, Soo glanced in the window one last time. She watched as one man spoke to the other, then turned and kept pace with them as they walked along the street.

There was no doubt in her mind.

They were being followed.

34

Two Targets

A SOFT DING announced the team's arrival at the twentieth floor. The mirrored elevator doors parted, revealing the Presidential Suite.

Rigor, Jules, and Kyla followed Matt and Kurien as they wheeled the large cases out of the elevator and across the opulent marble floor.

"Damn," Rigor said. "So, this is how the other half lives."

Kurien laughed. "This is nothing," he replied. "No offense to my friend, but the Grand Vladivostok pales in comparison to high-end hotels in Moscow. This is... how you say... slumming it."

"If this is slumming it," Kyla said, "I could get used to this level of poor."

"Same here," Jules added.

Matt got straight to work removing the weapons from

the cases. "Leave the HALO gear," he said. "We'll take it with us when we leave. For now, keep your MK close enough to reach it if you have to." He removed his pistol and sound suppressor from the crate, released the weapon's magazine, inspected it. Full. Satisfied, he slammed the mag back into the gun's handgrip and set it down on a nearby table.

The team followed suit, checked their weapons.

Matt removed his parachuting jumpsuit from the crate, rifled through its inside pockets, removed the ancillary armaments he had taken from the agency's secret hangar in Barbados: the combination auto-injector pen and IED; the round fake pill container which held one hundred feet of micro-thin explosive Detcord; two ceramic knives. He spoke to his team. "We'll gear up later. Right now, we're going shopping."

Jules, Kyla, and Rigor removed their gear from the pockets of their jumpsuits, plus the pairs of silver earrings which doubled as twin-bladed throwing stars. Kyla held the deadly fashion accessory up to her ear, checked her look in the vestibule mirror. "Beautiful," she said. "Whoever came up with this knows what a girl likes."

Jules nodded. "Bring on the bling."

"You got that right," Kyla replied.

Matt turned to Kurien. "Alexander, you'll remain here. Keep the room locked down until we get back."

Kurien nodded. "Will do."

Matt held up his auto injector / IED pen, addressed the team. "Remember what I said about this pen. To render someone unconscious, rotate the sleeve and press down on the orange end cap. The thrust tube located below the cap is spring-loaded. It will dispense a single dose of liquid halothane from the reservoir into your adversary's bloodstream, which will render them unconscious. The purple sleeve on the other end carries an explosive charge. Twist the sleeve once, toss the pen, then take cover. You've got five seconds before the RX-27 blast gel inside it goes boom. I suggest using the explosive option as a last resort. The less noise we make, the faster we can get out of here without drawing attention to ourselves. We'll extract Dr. Park at our first opportunity. Got it?"

The team nodded.

"All right," Matt said. "Let's go pick up a few things."

THE TEAM REACHED the lobby just as Soo, Tam, and Minho entered the hotel. Rigor removed his phone, brought up her picture. "That's our target," he said. "That's Dr. Park."

"Copy that," Matt replied.

As mother and son walked past, Matt stepped away from the group. "Wait here," he said.

He removed his phone, turned, walked casually towards the elevator, and stopped.

A second later, he heard Rigor's voice in his earbud. "Looks like they're being followed. Two males in suits. Look North Korean to me, probably RGB. On your six in three, two..."

Matt turned away as the two men walked past, then casually turned back. He watched the family board the elevator and the doors close behind them.

The men stopped, watched the elevator leave the ground floor, then took a seat in the lobby.

Matt watched as the numbers on the elevator display

changed, then pocketed his phone, left the hotel, and rejoined his team outside.

"Dr. Park is on the tenth floor," he said.

"There was a boy and a dog with her," Rigor said. "What's up with that?"

Matt shook his head. "I don't know. That wasn't part of the intel package."

"Well, it sure as shit is now."

Matt nodded. "I know."

"How do you want to handle it?" Kyla asked.

Jules interjected. "If the boy is her son, there's no way she's leaving here without him."

"This op just got a lot more challenging," Rigor added. "We no longer have a single target to extract. We have two."

"Plus, she's protected," Kyla said. "If she's being shadowed by the two RGB operatives we saw, you can be sure there are more. There's no way a scientist of her importance is being covered solely by a two-person detail."

"We need to nail down an extraction plan, and fast," Rigor said. "This place will be buzzing with conference delegates and security personnel by tomorrow. Got any ideas?"

Matt nodded. "Yeah."

"What did you have in mind?" Kyla asked.

"We move up our timeline," Matt replied. "We take Dr. Park tonight."

35

No Fun At All

SOO, TAM, AND Minho returned to their room. Soo opened the hotel door quietly and put her finger to her lips. "Shh," she said. "Gran's sleeping."

Minho raced into the room, jumped onto the bed, then subjected the family matriarch to an onslaught of wet doggy kisses.

Gran pushed the dog away. "Minho!" she objected. "Leave me alone!"

Minho chuffed playfully, then resumed his attack. Finally, Gran began to laugh. "Okay, okay! I'm awake!"

Soo hurried to her mother's aid, grabbed Minho's collar, eased him off the bed. "Sorry, Mom," she said. "We were trying not to wake you. Apparently, Minho had other ideas."

Gran sat up. Soo fluffed her pillows, made her more comfortable, helped her lie back. "It's all right," she said.

"I'm used to it. You're the only one the dog lets sleep in." She patted the bedside with her hand. "Come, grandson. Sit. Tell me all about your day."

Tam sat beside his grandmother. "It was cool," he said excitedly. "We checked out a huge department store, almost got kicked out by the security guard, made a run for it, and got away, then we watched how candy is made. It was epic!"

Gran laughed. "First cool, now epic. Sounds like you had quite a time."

Tam nodded. "We did! Minho and I wanted to keep going and check out more stores, but Mom got tired, so we came back."

"I told you, Tam," Soo said. "I have a function to attend tonight. I can't arrive there tired."

"It's okay," Tam replied. "I get it. You're old. You tire easily."

Soo crossed her arms. "I'm *what*?"

"Old," Tam replied. "Not as old as Gran, but still old."

Gran smiled. "You're right, grandson. Your mother is old, very old. She's practically an antique."

"Okay you two, knock it off," Soo replied with a smile. She pulled down her bed's comforter, drew down the top sheet. "Watch TV if you want, but I'm going to sleep for a couple of hours. Tonight's meet and greet is for delegates only, so I'll be attending the function alone. Call room service and order whatever you want for dinner. I don't know how long the event will be, but I'm guessing at least a few hours. Formal presentations commence at nine o'clock tomorrow morning, so everyone will need to be in bed at a reasonable hour. That includes you three."

Minho hopped up into a tub chair in the corner of the

room, turned himself around several times, then relaxed into a ball. He let out a heavy sigh.

"See?" Soo said. "Even Minho is tired, and he has nowhere to be tonight."

Tam turned on the television, flipped through the channels, found nothing of interest to watch. He walked to the window, looked out. In the distance, he observed the freighters as they entered and exited the Port of Vladivostok.

"Mom?" he asked.

"Hmm?" Soo replied.

"Can we go to the docks tomorrow and check out the ships?"

"Sure, hon," Soo said sleepily. "If there's time."

"Cool."

"Mom?"

No response.

"Mom?" Tam repeated.

Soo snored lightly.

Tam turned to Minho. "What'd I tell ya, boy? *Old*."

Minho yawned. Seconds later, he too began to snore.

Tam shook his head, whispered. "You guys are no fun at all."

36

Not On The Register

THE TEAM WRAPPED up their shopping spree and returned to the Presidential Suite. They would now be suitably dressed for the evening.

Rigor turned to Matt. "You said you wanted to take Dr. Park tonight?"

Matt nodded. "Correct."

"How do you propose we do that? Building security will be tighter than a bull's butt during fly season, not to mention Park's shadow security detail and the boys from the FSB and RGB running around."

"I have an idea," Matt replied. "But first I have to do a little recon."

"You want backup?"

Matt shook his head. "No. I want you and Jules to stay in

the room and off the radar until tonight. That goes for you too, Alexander."

Kurien nodded. "As you wish."

"Stay on comms," Matt said. "When the time is right, you'll know it." He turned to Jules. "I need you to put your computer skills to work."

"Sure," Jules replied. "What do you need?"

"When we saw Dr. Park enter the hotel she was in the company of a boy and a dog. Hack into the hotel reservations program. Find out if anyone else is registered in her party."

"On it," Jules replied. She walked away, removed her phone, and began to type.

"I'm going to change," Matt said to Kyla. "Care to join me for a walk around the hotel?"

Kyla smiled. "Can I wear my new dress and shoes?"

"Of course."

Several minutes later, Matt and Kyla walked out of the bedroom. Rigor whistled. "Damn, girl," he said. "You're making that dress beg for mercy!"

Jules looked up from her phone. "He's right, Kyla. You look gorgeous."

Kyla curtsied. "Why, thank you. Thank you very much."

Matt opened his arms. "Hey, what about me?"

Rigor shrugged. "Not bad."

"Not bad? This suit cost two thousand bucks!"

"Sorry, brother," Rigor replied. "I'm partial to a lady in a dress. Especially when it's *that* dress."

Matt pointed. "You realize your girlfriend is sitting right there."

Jules laughed. "Don't worry about it, Matt. You know

how many hotties we get on the dive boat each year? Hundreds. The big man's all talk and no action."

Kyla walked over to Rigor, gave him a peck on the cheek. "Thank you just the same, handsome."

Rigor smiled. "You're welcome. But I have a question."

"What's that?" Kyla asked.

"You carrying?"

Kyla played with her moon-shaped earrings. "I am. Plus another weapon hidden somewhere I'm not going to show you."

Rigor chuckled. "Copy that."

"And yes, Matt," Jules said. "You look very nice, too. Every bit the business executive."

"Thanks, Jules," Matt said.

"Nice is pushing it," Rigor teased. "Acceptable is more like it."

Matt turned to Kyla. "Ready to roll, sexy?"

Kyla smiled, took Matt's hand in hers. "You bet."

MATT AND KYLA rode the elevator down to the mezzanine, exited the car, strolled through the lobby.

Jules came on comms and spoke to Matt in his earbud. "I have an update on Dr. Park," she said.

Matt stopped, hugged Kyla, replied. "And?"

"She's traveling with her son, mother, and their family dog. They're in suite 1006."

Matt stroked Kyla's hair. "Anything else?"

"Yes. I downloaded her itinerary. She's attending a meet and greet tonight. Delegates only."

"Time?"

"Seven o'clock."

"Where?"

"Here. Third floor. Room C. Regency Hall."

"Heading there now."

"Copy."

THE THIRD FLOOR elevator doors parted. Matt and Kyla stepped out. Matt whispered. "Follow my lead."

"Copy," Kyla said. She stopped to observe the artwork on the wall outside Regency Hall, called Matt's attention to it as the catering staff milled about. "Beautiful, isn't it?" she commented.

Matt nodded. "It is."

Kyla casually glanced up and down the hallway. "Two operatives on my left," she said. "Probably more in the room."

"Why don't we go inside and look around?" Matt said.

Kyla slipped her arm into Matt's. "Sounds good."

Within seconds of entering the room, they were met by a Russian in his early twenties. He raised his hand, stopped them. "I'm sorry," he said. "This room is closed to the public for a private function."

"I trust the setup is going well?" Matt asked.

"Excuse me?" the man replied.

"My apologies," Matt said. He reached into his pocket, removed his business card, presented it. The man read the company name aloud. "Global Confectioners, Barbados. You're a long way from home."

Matt laughed. "Yes, I am. My company is one of the

world's finest purveyors of luxury chocolate. We're providing the sweet table for tonight's event."

"Sweet table?"

Matt nodded. "Assorted gourmet chocolates, a chocolate dipping fountain, plus post-event gifts for the attendees."

The man stared at Matt's card. "Are you on the register?"

Matt crossed his arms, appeared offended, replied briskly. "On the register? My company does not deal with *registers*. Do you mean to tell me you've never heard of Global Confectioners?"

The man shrugged. "Sorry."

Matt sighed. "I see. Perhaps I should speak to your supervisor."

"Why would you need to do that?"

"Because it's apparent that the event staff, which includes you, is ill prepared. Of all the companies contributing to tonight's function, you should have known my company by name. I'm truly offended." Matt pointed to a draped and skirted banquet table located across the room in front of a massive picture window. "Come with me," he said. "Let me show you something."

The man hesitated, then followed Matt across the room. "Show me what?"

Kyla glanced over her shoulder. The room was now set up for the evening's event. She watched as the last staff member left the room and closed the double doors behind him.

Matt walked behind the banquet table to the window, looked down, pointed to the street below. "There," he said. "Do you see that?"

The Russian stepped forward, looked down. "I don't see what you're—"

Matt removed the injector pen from his jacket pocket, placed it against the man's neck, pressed the plunger.

The man fell into his arms, unconscious.

Matt lowered him to the ground, slipped him under the skirted banquet table, tucked his body out of sight. "He won't be waking up until midnight," he said to Kyla. "Go to the door. Keep an eye open. I'll be there in a second."

Kyla nodded. "Copy that."

As Kyla hurried away, Matt removed the small case of microfilament Detcord from his pants pocket, ran a thin strip of the explosive along the windowsill, pressed it into place, then walked across the room to join Kyla.

"We're good," he said. He opened the door, looked around.

The hall was empty.

"Let's get out of here."

"Copy that," Kyla replied.

They headed for the elevator.

37

A Toast

SOO CHECKED HER hair and makeup one last time, then stepped out of the bathroom into the main suite. "Well, what do you think?"

Tam sat on the floor, watching television. Minho lay beside him, stretched out, enjoying a belly rub. Upon hearing the bathroom door open, the dog looked up, wagged his tail.

Gran sat in a chair watching television with her grandson.

"Whoa," Tam said. "Mom, you look amazing!"

The simple black cocktail dress hugged her figure, accentuated her natural curves. She fiddled with the dress, pulled it lower.

"It's perfect, my dear," Gran said. "You look beautiful."

Soo sighed nervously. "It's not too short?"

"The length is perfectly acceptable," Gran said. "Just right."

"Yeah," Tam said. "Check it out. Mom's got legs!"

Gran warned the boy. "You're too young to be noticing a woman's legs, Tam."

"I may be young, Gran," Tam replied. "But I'm not blind."

Minho stared at Soo, panted, slapped his tail repeatedly against the floor.

"See?" Tam said. "Minho thinks so too."

Soo smiled. "Thank you, Minho."

"You're going to take every man's mind off the conference and make them forget the reason they're here," Gran said.

Soo shook her head. "I wouldn't be so sure about that."

Gran winked. "I would."

"You're just saying that because I'm your daughter."

Gran rose from her chair, walked to Soo, held her face in her hands. "No, honey," she said. "I'm saying it because it's true."

"I'm nowhere near ready for that," Soo replied solemnly. "I won't be for some time."

Gran sighed. "I know how hard it is to lose the one you love," she replied. "But there comes a time when you know you've grieved long enough and that it's okay to move on."

A knock on their room door interrupted their conversation.

Soo walked to the door, looked through the peephole, stepped back. "Oh my," she said.

"What is it?" Gran asked. "Who's there?"

"It's Dr. Kim."

Gran's face lit up. She broke into a wide grin. "You mean Dr. Sexy Butt?"

"Mom!"

"Oh pish posh, daughter," she exclaimed. "Don't just stand there. Greet the man!"

Soo composed herself, opened the door. "Dr. Kim," she said. "Hello."

Kim smiled. "Good evening, Dr. Park. I hope presenting myself at your door unannounced doesn't constitute an intrusion."

"No," Soo replied. "Of course not."

Dr. Kim was smartly dressed in a simple black tuxedo, white shirt, bow tie, and shiny patent leather shoes. He cleared his throat nervously. "I was wondering if you might join me this evening. I know tonight's event is a business mixer, but I was hoping it might also give us an opportunity to get to know each other a little better. If you're agreeable to that, of course."

Unseen, Gran called out from the room. "She'd love to!"

Soo rolled her eyes, smiled at Dr. Kim. "That voice belongs to my snoopy mother."

Dr. Kim laughed. He called into the room. "Good evening, ma'am."

Gran came to the door. "Good evening, doctor," she said. She looked Dr. Kim up and down approvingly. "My, my. Aren't you dapper!"

Soo blushed, shot her mother a warning look. "*Mom!*"

Dr. Kim smiled. "Thank you," he replied. "That's very nice of you to say."

Gran winked. "I just call 'em as I see 'em."

Dr. Kim turned his attention back to Soo. "What do you say, Dr. Park? Care to join me tonight?"

Soo smiled. "It would be my pleasure."

"Excellent," Kim said. "Are you ready? Do you need a little more time?"

"Oh, she's ready," Gran said.

Soo sighed. "We should leave before my mother embarrasses me any further."

Dr. Kim laughed. He offered Soo his arm. "Shall we go?"

Soo retrieved her clutch purse from a side table near the front door, slipped her arm through Dr. Kim's. "We shall," she replied.

Gran called out as they walked toward the elevator. "Stay out as long as you want, sweetheart. I've got everything under control."

Soo called back. "Thank you, mother. Unnecessary, but thank you."

Dr. Kim laughed.

DR. KIM WAITED for Soo to exit the elevator. Outside the Regency ballroom, the hallway was buzzing with activity. The ballroom doors remained closed and locked.

"May I ask a favor, Dr. Park?" he asked.

Soo turned. "Of course."

"Unless we're in the company of our colleagues, perhaps we could dispense with addressing each other formally. My name is Kyu."

Soo smiled. "Soo."

"That's a beautiful name," Kyu said. "It suits you."

Soo felt her face blush. "Thank you."

Kyu stopped a server as she approached, removed two glasses of champagne from her tray, handed one to Soo. "Champagne?"

Soo accepted the glass.

Kyu raised his glass, proposed a toast. "To the women of science and their remarkable discoveries."

Soo smiled. "Thank you. That was very nice."

"You're welcome."

The pair chatted as they meandered through the crowd.

"When we first met," Soo said, "you mentioned that you would be presenting an award at the end of the conference."

Kyu nodded. "That's correct. The National Medal of Distinction."

"I've never heard of it before," Soo said. "Is it a new honor?"

"Most definitely. This year's recipient will be the first to receive it."

"What does it signify?"

"It is the country's most prestigious award for scientific achievement. You and Dr. Cho are strong contenders to receive it."

"Should you be telling me that?"

Kyu smiled, sipped his champagne. "I may have provided you with a little more information than I should have."

"Meaning?"

"The presentation was to have been a surprise. I was to announce the creation of the award and confer it upon its first recipient at tomorrow night's dinner and gala."

"I'm sure that will be a very exciting moment for everyone."

Kyu nodded. "Indeed, it will."

Soo observed the growing crowd. The hallway had become packed. "I hope they open the doors and let us in soon," she said.

"I agree," Kyu said. "Give me a second. I'll make an inquiry."

"Sounds good."

As Kyu walked away, Soo heard her name being called. She turned. Jin Cho stood in front of her.

"Jin," she said.

"Soo, we need to talk," Jin said.

"You should have called my room earlier, Jin. I don't feel comfortable having this discussion with you here."

"I do," Jin said. "My colleague and best friend believes I did something wrong when I did nothing of the sort."

"I found the listening device in Minho's toy, Jin. You gave it to me to give to my dog. You knew it would end up in my house."

"Do you think for a moment that is something I would do willingly?"

"You might."

"Of course not. I was *made* to do it."

"What are you talking about?"

"Last week, I was picked up by the RGB. They interviewed me, asked me questions about you, about your brother and our relationship, both inside and outside of the lab. I told them I knew nothing, and that if they wanted answers to their questions, they needed to speak to you directly because I knew you had nothing to hide. I would never do anything to hurt you or your family, Soo. Believe me or not. I'll leave that up to you." Jin opened her purse, removed a thumb drive, handed it to Soo. "You said you wanted a copy of my presentation to review before tomorrow. Here it is." She sighed. "That's it. I said what I wanted to say. Have a good night."

Jin turned and walked away.

Soo watched her go. There was a conviction in her voice unlike any she had heard before.

She was telling the truth.

Soo recalled the men who had been watching her and Tam from across the street earlier in the day, and the car which she and her mother had witnessed parked down the road from their house for the past week. The situation became clear.

The RGB was surveilling her.

The doors to the Regency ballroom opened. Guests began entering the room.

Across the room, Soo saw Kyu wave.

She slipped the thumb drive into her clutch, waved back, headed for the Regency ballroom.

She suddenly felt very exposed.

And in danger.

38

Anwoo Kang

THE TEAM EXITED the third-floor elevator and mixed with the crowd as they entered the ornately decorated Regency ballroom. Hundreds of flags representing North Korea and Russia hung from the ceiling. Eight-foot round tables with seating for ten dotted the room, each covered with a white linen tablecloth, skirted to the floor. Music played through the ceiling speakers, the song choices alternating between Russian and North Korean state songs. Ice sculptures of famous Russian and North Korean landmarks anchored the open bar at the end of the room.

Soo took in the beauty of the room. She turned to Kyu. "This is incredible," she said.

Kyu nodded. "It certainly is."

"I've never seen anything like it. The ice sculptures are magnificent. We don't have anything like that back home."

"I'm sorry to hear that," Kyu said.

Soo looked at him strangely. "What do you mean?"

Kyu corrected himself. "I'm sorry. I misspoke. What I meant to say is that we too should have such art to appreciate. An ice sculpture is such a simple thing. I'm surprised our Supreme Leader has not seen fit to make such displays public attractions. Our people would enjoy it as much as the Russians."

Soo nodded. "Yes, they would."

RIGOR AND JULES mingled with the guests. Rigor spoke to Matt through his communications earbud. "I have Dr. Park," he said. "She's talking to some dude. Can't tell if she knows him or if she's just engaging in pleasant conversation. Where are you?"

Matt responded. "Kyla and I are at the bar."

"Bring me a Scotch, will ya? Neat."

"Sorry, pal," Matt replied. "No drinking on the job."

"We're supposed to fit in, aren't we?"

"I'll bring you a ginger ale, straight up."

"On the rocks."

"Copy that. Jules?"

"Go ahead, Matt."

"I need you to find out who Dr. Park is talking to."

"No problem. You and Kyla make your way over to her. Leave the rest to me."

"Copy."

"YOU MENTIONED you have been reviewing the work of all the Nest teams," Soo asked. "Which has impressed you the most?"

Kyu crossed his arms, pondered the question. "That's a difficult question to answer."

"Why?"

"Because the work of each Nest differs so greatly from one to the next."

"But you've researched them all, right? You'd have to do that before deciding upon a winner."

"I have."

"I'm impressed. It couldn't have been easy finding a worthy recipient for the Medal of Dominion."

"It wasn't."

"How long is the vetting process?"

"I've been assessing the work of each group for the past year."

"And you report to whom?"

Kyu paused. "Sorry?"

"Each Nest reports to a different representative of the State. It's a national security requirement. Who is your representative?"

Kyu smiled. "I'm not sure if I should tell you that."

"My apologies if I've crossed a line," Soo said. "I'm sorry. It's just that I find what you do to be fascinating. To have a front-row seat to every project in development at all the Nest's? For me, that would be a dream come true. Don't get me wrong. I love the work that I do in research. But it's so narrowly focused. I would consider it an honor to see the operations of the State from such a broader perspective."

"I do," Kyu replied.

Soo tipped back the last of her champagne. "Boy," she said, "That has a bit of a kick to it!"

Kyu laughed. "Better go easy on that stuff. We still have the whole night ahead of us."

"Just don't keep me out past my bedtime or my mother will have a fit."

"You're a big girl. I'm sure your mother won't mind."

"No, but my son will."

Kyu nodded. "Point taken."

MATT AND KYLA walked through the crowd, stopped beside Soo and the unknown man.

Rigor and Jules called out, walked up to Matt and Kyla. Jules leaned in, gave Kyla a warm hug, whispered. "Say cheese, you two."

Matt put his arm around Kyla and smiled.

Jules snapped their picture with her phone.

"Got it," she said. "Give me a second."

"Thanks," Matt replied.

Rigor, Matt, and Kyla conversed while Jules ran the image of the man Soo was speaking to through a special agency app on her phone. The program's facial recognition database found a match. "We have a problem, Matt," she said.

"What's that?" Matt asked.

"The name on the card in the guy's lanyard says it's Dr. Kyu-Ho Kim. His real name is Anwoo Kang. He's an operative with South Korea's First Bureau Signature Intelligence

Unit, National Intelligence Service. You know what that means, right?"

"He's not here for the shrimp cocktail?" Rigor asked.

Jules shook her head. "No, he's not. He's here for Dr. Park."

"Which means he's not alone," Kyla added. "He's part of an extraction team."

Matt nodded. "Looks like South Korea wants the Synoxin-9 formula as much as we do."

"YOU KNOW, I could really go for another glass of champagne," Soo said. "Would you mind?"

Kyu nodded. "Of course. I'll be right back."

Soo called after him. "Make sure it's nice and cold."

Kyu smiled. "Will do."

Soo began to panic. Something was definitely wrong. She walked toward the exit door, then stopped as two men blocked her path. The look in their eyes told her they were with Kyu. She recognized one of the men, had seen him earlier in the day. He and his partner had positioned themselves across the street from the candy store. He carried himself like a man who had seen much conflict in his life and could carry himself in a fight. She returned to the middle of the ballroom, searched the room for Jin, saw her seated at a table on the opposite side of the room. She had to get to her, to warn her they were in danger.

"One ice cold glass of champagne," Kyu said. "Just as the lady requested."

Soo turned around, a look of surprise on her face. "My, that was fast."

"You okay?" Kyu asked.

Soo accepted the drink, replied nervously. "Sorry?"

Kyu laughed. "You look like you just saw a ghost."

Soo said nothing.

"What is it?" Kyu asked. "What's wrong?"

Soo took a deep breath. "Who are you?" she asked.

Kyu looked perplexed. "Who am I? What do you mean?"

"You know what I mean."

"I'm afraid I don't."

"You're not here to present an award, are you?"

"What's gotten into you, Soo?" Kyu asked. "Of course, I am."

"The Medal of Dominion?"

Kyu nodded. "That's correct."

"That's not what you called it when we first met."

"What are you talking about?"

"You called it the Medal of *Distinction*, not Dominion. Surely you'd know the correct name of the award, wouldn't you?"

Kyu said nothing.

"I also told you that each Nest reports to a different representative of the State. You never challenged that statement. That's not true. There is only one representative that accepts the reports for all Nests, and no one knows who that person is... *for reasons of national security*."

Kyu nodded. "I'm impressed."

"Answer my question," Soo said. "Who are you?"

"I'll share that information with you when we're out of this room," Kyu replied. He looked around the room, spotted his men, and waved them over.

The men joined him.

"Please escort Dr. Park to her room," he instructed. "Do

it quietly." He turned to Soo. "I suggest you do exactly as you're told from here on."

"And if I don't?" Soo replied briskly.

"That would be unwise."

"I could scream."

"You could," Kyu agreed. He removed his cell phone. "But the second you do, I'll place a call to my colleagues. They're waiting for us outside your room. You wouldn't want anything to happen to your mother or your son, would you? Or your dog?"

"You wouldn't dare."

"That's entirely up to you."

A shiver ran through Soo's body. "All right," she said. "I'll leave with you. Just don't hurt my family."

"Smart decision." Kyu addressed his men. "Let's go."

Together, the South Korean operatives escorted Soo out of the ballroom.

39

This Ought To Be Interesting

MATT WATCHED Anwoo Kang and his men escort Soo out of the Regency ballroom. He spoke to his team as he watched them walk to the elevator. "The two operatives we saw in the lobby who were shadowing Dr. Park and her family are behind us. If Kang's men realize who they are, it'll be a bloodbath. We can't afford to have Dr. Park hurt. Rigor and Jules, deal with them. Kyla and I will stay with the asset."

"Copy that," Rigor replied. "Jules, on me."

Rigor and Jules hurried ahead. Rigor tapped the older operative on his shoulder. "Excuse me," he said.

The RGB operative stopped. "Yes?" he said.

Rigor pointed. "Are you aware that your jacket pocket is torn?"

As the operative glanced down at his pocket, Rigor activated his auto-injector pen, pressed it against the man's leg, clicked the plunger.

Jules walked up behind the younger operative as he waited for his partner, injected a dose of liquid halothane into his back.

The two men responded to the drug immediately, lost their balance.

Rigor and Jules grabbed the men as they fell, then helped them to a nearby table as concerned attendees looked on.

Rigor smiled, addressed the small group. "It's okay, folks," he said. "Nothing to see here. These two just hit the bar a little too hard."

As Rigor dealt with the older man, Jules helped the younger operative into a chair, laid his head on the tabletop. "You'll be fine," she whispered. "Nighty-night."

Rigor communicated with Matt. "We're good. Coming to you."

They exited the ballroom, watched as the elevator doors fell closed ahead of Matt and Kyla.

"We missed them," Kyla reported. "Dr. Park is in the elevator with Kang and his men." She watched the numbers on the LCD display above the car rise rapidly, then stop. "They're on 10."

"That's Dr. Park's floor," Matt said. "Kang must be taking her to her family, using them as leverage. Rigor, Jules, get up there. Protect the family at all costs."

"On it," Rigor replied. He removed his pistol from his waistband at the small of his back, took a sound suppressor from his jacket pocket, attached the silencer to the weapon, and hid the gun under his jacket. "Jules and I will take the stairs and approach from opposite ends of the floor. Watch your crossfire."

"Copy that," Kyla replied. She pressed the elevator call button, waited for the car to arrive, entered with Matt, tapped the button for the tenth floor. Matt waited for the doors to close. "Cover your ears," he said. He removed the fake pill container from his pocket. "This is going to get loud."

As the elevator ascended, Matt clicked the container lid three times.

Inside the Regency ballroom, the RF signal reached the thin strip of Detcord Matt had run along the windowsill beneath the room's massive picture window.

The window exploded with an incredible *boom*.

Outside the Grand Vladivostok, fragments of shattered glass rained down from the building. Pedestrians walking along the sidewalk below covered their heads and ran for cover as they tried to protect themselves from the falling glass.

Screams emanated from inside the Regency ballroom. The sound of the chaos grew fainter as the elevator carried Matt and Kyla up and away from the source of the explosion to the tenth floor.

"That should provide us with the distraction we'll need," Matt said as the elevator came to a gentle stop.

Kyla removed her gun from her clutch purse, screwed on the silencer, chambered a round, nodded. "Let's hope so."

"Follow my lead," Matt said. "When you hear me speak, I'll be in position. Make your move then."

Kyla nodded, kept out of sight of the opening doors,

NOMAD

waited for Matt to step onto the floor. He held his key card
in his hand, looked down the hallway, saw the two operatives standing several doors down outside suite 1006, walked
in their direction, then purposely dropped his key card.
"Shit," he said. He leaned down to pick it up.

Upon hearing Matt's voice, Kyla exited the elevator,
pistol raised. She targeted the two operatives. Distracted by
Matt, the men fumbled for their weapons, but it was already
too late.

Kyla advanced on them quickly, squeezed off two rapid
silenced rounds, both headshots.

Thwup, thwup.

Matt ran forward, caught the men as they fell, eased
their bodies to the ground, dragged them away from the
threshold of the Park's door. He looked at Kyla, raised a
finger to his lips.

Kyla nodded.

Matt placed his ear to the door, listened. From inside the
suite came the sound of faint cries and low voices.

A dog growled.

The emergency exit doors at the end of the hallway
opened. Rigor and Jules appeared at opposite ends of the
hallway, guns drawn. Slowly, they made their way to Matt
and Kyla, then turned, each covering one end of the
hallway.

Matt whispered to Rigor, pointed to one of the dead
men. "Give me a hand with this guy."

"What for?" Rigor said. He observed the hole in the
man's forehead. "He's done."

"Yeah, but he's still useful."

"How do you figure?"

203

"He's going to get us into Park's room."

"A dead guy's gonna do that?"

Matt nodded. "Lift him up, walk him to the door, then turn his head away from the peephole."

Rigor shrugged. "This ought to be interesting."

The men lifted the dead operative's body, carried him to the door. Rigor stayed low, lifted the man to eye level with the peephole. Matt positioned the man's head to the side, making it impossible to see the hole in his forehead, then stepped aside. He turned to Kyla and Jules, mouthed the words: Ready?

The women nodded, raised their weapons, waited.

Matt knocked on the door.

No response.

Knocked again.

A voice replied from inside the suite. "What is it?"

The team waited.

The light inside the room which brightened the peephole suddenly fell dark.

Matt heard the door's security latch disengage. A man spoke angrily as he opened the door. "I told you I was not to be disturb—"

Rigor pushed the dead man's body through the doorway, let the corpse fall onto the marble floor.

Caught off guard, Anwoo Kang tumbled backward, lost his balance, fell, watched his weapon skitter away from him across the floor. He glanced at the gun, then stared up at Rigor.

Rigor drew his weapon, bent down, buried its muzzle into Kang's forehead. "Go ahead," he said. "Give me a fucking reason."

Kang relaxed, presented his empty hands to Rigor.

"Get up," Rigor said. He leaned over, grabbed the National Intelligence Service operative by his tuxedo lapel, yanked him to his feet. "Who are you supposed to be?" Rigor asked as he patted him down, checked him for additional weapons. "South Korea's answer to James Bond?"

Kang watched as Matt, Kyla, and Jules entered the room behind Rigor, their weapons drawn.

He smiled. "You've made a big mistake by coming here."

Matt stepped past the South Korean operative, walked to Soo. "Are you all right, Dr. Park?" he asked.

Soo nodded. "I am."

Matt looked around the room. "And your family? Is everyone safe?"

Gran stepped forward. "What is the meaning of this?" she asked. "Do you have any idea who my daughter is?"

Matt nodded. "Yes, ma'am," he replied. "We do." He glanced at Tam. "How about you, young man? You good?"

Tam nodded.

Sensing no threat from the intruders, Minho walked up to Matt, sniffed his leg. Matt scratched the dog's head. "Good boy," he said.

Minho wagged his tail, panted.

"Who are you?" Soo asked. "What is all this about?"

"My team and I are with American Intelligence, Dr. Park. We've come to take you to your brother."

Soo brought her hand to her mouth. "Hyon made it? He's alive?"

Matt nodded. "He is."

"Where is he?"

"I'm afraid I can't tell you that," Matt replied. "Just know that he's in our custody and he's safe. Our mission is to extract you from the conference and bring you to him."

Soo replied hastily. "What do you need us to do?"

"Follow our commands to the letter."

"Of course."

"And give us everything you have on Synoxin-9."

Soo paused. "If I do that, my family and I are dead."

Matt pointed to Kang. Rigor held him in a firm grasp, his big hand practically encircling the man's neck. "He's the one you have to worry about, Dr. Park, not us. He's with South Korean National Intelligence. Your brother is not in their custody. He's in ours. He and his men came here to take you to South Korea and put you to work for them. My guess is you'd be leaving here alone, never to see your family again. Their plan was to kill them while you watched." Matt turned to Kang. "Tell her I'm wrong."

Kang shook his head. "You and your people will never get out of this hotel alive. I have men watching for Dr. Park. If our operation goes wrong, they have orders to shoot to kill."

Matt turned back to Soo. "Did you hear what he just said? Shoot to kill. I promise you we'll do everything in our power to keep you safe. I just need you to trust us. Can you do that?"

Soo nodded. "We can."

"Good," Matt said. "Grab only what is important. Passports, ID, your computer, everything related to your research. We'll take care of the rest."

"What about my family... and Minho?"

Matt shook his head. "I didn't see them as being part of the plan, but they are now."

"I won't go anywhere without them," Soo said firmly.

"Understood. Now hurry."

Soo ran into her bedroom.

Kang's cell phone chirped.

Rigor opened the operative's tuxedo jacket, removed the phone from his inside pocket, checked the text display of Korean characters, handed it to Jules. "What does it say?"

Jules read the text message. "Someone from his team is asking where he and Dr. Park are."

"You'd better reply, Jules," Matt said.

"What do you want me to say?"

"Anything that will buy us time."

Jules nodded. "Copy that."

As she typed, the hotel's emergency alarm sounded. *BEEP... BEEP... BEEP...*

Kang laughed. "Good luck getting out of here now. That's the evacuation alarm. In a few minutes, this place will be swarming with fire and police. And when my men see you with Dr. Park and her family, you're all dead."

"You know what?" Rigor asked the operative.

"What?" Kang replied.

"You're beginning to get on my nerves." Rigor squeezed his hand tightly around Kang's neck, watched as the man struggled under his constricting grip. Soon, Kang's body fell limp.

Soo returned to the room in time to see Rigor release the man and watch him fall to the floor. "Is he dead?" she asked.

Rigor shook his head. "Nah, just taking a nap. Smug little prick."

Jules finished texting the reply. "There," she said. "That should do it."

"Good," Matt said. "Bring Kang's phone. You ready, Dr. Park?"

Soo nodded.

"Kyla, Jules, check the hallway," Matt ordered.

Kyla opened the door, stepped out. Jules followed. "Clear," Kyla said.

"Let's go," Matt said.

The frightened family and their dog followed the team out of their room to the emergency stairwell. Together they hurried up the stairs to the safety of the twentieth floor.

40

Promise Me One Thing

RIGOR CARRIED SOO'S mother in his arms as the team and the family made their way up the stairs to the twentieth floor. He lowered her to her feet when they reached the landing. "You okay, ma'am?" he asked.

"I haven't been carried like that for a very long time," Gran replied. She winked. "Wanna go again?"

Rigor blushed. "Maybe later."

Matt touched his key card against the electronic lock reader, listened as the lock disengaged, raised his weapon to eye level, opened the steel door a crack, peeked through.

The hallway was empty.

"On me," he said.

Matt threw open the door, hurried along the corridor,

reached their suite, tapped the key card against the lock pad, opened the door. "Everybody inside," he said. "Quickly!"

Alexander Kurien stood aside as the family and Minho ran into the room, followed by the team. "Are you all right?" he asked.

Matt nodded. "We ran into a little trouble. Nothing we couldn't handle."

"I heard an explosion," Kurien said. "It shook the windows. Then the emergency alarm sounded. Was that you?"

Matt removed his tie, tossed it on the couch, unbuttoned his shirt collar. "I may have blown something up," he replied. "Couldn't be helped."

Kurien stared at the family and their dog. They looked frightened. "I thought we were only extracting Dr. Park," he said.

"You know what they say about plans," Matt replied. "Better off not making them."

Kurien looked perplexed. "The family *and* a dog?"

"They're a package deal."

"Think of it as no man left behind," Rigor added, "or, in this case, no family. Besides, Gran has a crush on me. Then again, how could she not?"

Kyla smiled.

Jules rolled her eyes.

"All right," Matt said. "Listen up. We need to get out of here. Alexander, did you bring the diplomatic tape with you?"

Kurien nodded. "It's in the case."

"Good," Matt replied. "Here's what we're going to do. Get the cases. Bring them here."

The team left the living room, returned seconds later, pushing the four large rolling cases in which they had stored their HALO gear and additional weapons. Matt unclipped their stainless steel hinges, lifted off the upper section, set it down. Rigor, Kyla, and Jules did the same.

Matt pulled the weapons and parachuting gear out of the case, dropped it on the floor. "We're going to rearrange things," he said. "First, we're going to get you settled in. I hope no one is claustrophobic."

"You want us to get in there?" Soo asked.

Matt nodded. "It'll only be for a few minutes. We need to get you down to our car. The hotel will be crawling with security by now, so you need to be out of sight."

"What about Minho?" Tam asked.

"He'll ride with you," Matt said. "He'll be quiet as long as you're with him to assure him that everything is all right."

Tam knelt down, petted Minho. "Hear that, boy?" he said. "You can't make a sound. Got it?"

The dog whined nervously, licked his master's face.

Tam looked up at Matt, smiled. "We're good."

"Attaboy," Matt replied. "Here's the deal. You hop into the case first. I'll lift Minho and put him in with you. Cool?"

"Cool," Tam replied.

"Good. Gran and Dr. Park, you'll each have your own case. The last case is for weapons and gear. Once you're inside, we'll lock the cases. Alexander will apply the diplomatic tape over the latches and seals. That way no one will be permitted to open them should we run into trouble before we get to the car. Got it?"

The team nodded.

"Okay, folks," Matt said. "All aboard."

Rigor eased Gran down into her case. "Are you comfortable, ma'am?" he asked.

Gran grinned. "I'd feel a lot safer if you were in here with me."

Rigor chuckled. "You must have been a handful back in the day."

Gran nodded. "I still am."

Rigor shook his head. "I don't doubt that for a second. You ready?"

Gran nodded. "Ready."

Rigor placed the lid over the box, secured its latches.

"Okay, Dr. Park," Matt said. "You're up."

Soo seated herself in the box. She raised her hand as Matt lowered the lid.

Matt hesitated. "Yes, Dr.?"

"If something goes wrong…" Soo said.

Matt shook his head. "Nothing is going to go wrong."

Soo insisted. "But if it does, promise me one thing."

"No need to ask," Matt replied. "We'll protect your family."

Soo sighed. "Thank you."

Matt smiled, lowered the lid, secured the latches.

Kurien tore off long strips of the diplomatic security tape, covered the latches, ran a length across the top of the crate. "There," he said. "Done."

"Good," Matt said.

The team rolled the cases to the elevator door. Matt pressed the call button, waited for the doors to open, rolled his case inside.

When all four cases had been moved into the elevator, Kurien pressed the call button for the lower level VIP parking, tapped his card key against the security pad. Access now granted, the VIP parking level button lit up.

The elevator and its precious cargo began its descent to the parking garage.

41

What Text?

ANWOO KANG CHOKED, coughed, and struggled to breathe as he came around. The vice-tight grip the American had applied to his throat had rendered him unconscious within seconds. He kept his head down, stared at the floor, concentrated on normalizing his breathing and regaining his senses. Confident that he could finally stand without falling, he pushed himself to his feet, felt the room begin to spin, made his way to a chair, sat down, looked around the room, remembered where he was.

The Park family suite.

Panic rushed over him. He looked around the room, saw his target was gone. He reached inside his tuxedo jacket, discovered his cell phone was missing, as was his weapon. Kang stood, glanced at the doorway, saw the body of one of his operatives lying face down on the vestibule, a pool of blood encircling his face. He stepped over the dead man, threw open the door, checked the hallway, saw his second operative lying on the ground, dead from a gunshot to the middle of his forehead. He rifled through the man's pockets, relieved him of his weapon and cell phone, placed a call.

"Where the hell are you?" the man answered. "Your text said you'd meet me here five minutes ago!"

"What text?" Kang replied. "I never sent you a text."

"I'm looking at it right now!"

"It didn't come from me."

"What are you talking about?"

"Never mind," Kang replied. "Park is gone. Another team is after her. Americans. We need to find them before they leave the hotel. Where are you now?"

"Outside the front entrance. The cops are moving everyone out of the hotel. I had no choice. I couldn't stay."

"Fuck!" Kang said. "All right. Keep an eye out for Park and her family. They'll be in the company of four Americans, two men and two women. If you see them, do not engage. We can't afford to get into a firefight in the middle of downtown. The police would be on us in no time. The car's parked across the street. Go to it and be ready for my call."

"Where are you going?"

"To check out the parking garage. The Americans had to have arrived by car. When I find them I'll call you."

"You sure you don't want me to slip back into the hotel and back you up?"

"No. I can handle the Americans. Besides, I have unfinished business with one of them."

"Unfinished business?"

"Never mind. Just do as I say."

"Copy."

Kang disconnected the call, walked down the hallway, ejected the magazine from the dead man's weapon, checked it. Full. He reinserted the mag, chambered a round. The poor bastard hadn't been able to squeeze off a single shot before he met his demise.

The elevator doors opened. Kang stepped inside, pressed the call button, waited impatiently as the car descended to the first parking level. He stepped out as the brushed aluminum doors parted, his weapon hidden behind his leg. The steady beeping from the emergency alarms located throughout the ceiling of the subterranean structure was deafening. The operative stopped, listened, heard voices close by. He walked to the corner, peered around it, and saw two police officers speaking to one another.

One of the officers glanced up, saw Kang, called out to him in Russian.

Kang ducked around the corner, swore to himself, decided how best to handle the situation.

The officer called out again.

Kang heard them as they began to walk in his direction. He stepped around the corner, faced them, stopped.

The officers kept their distance, called out again.

Kang shook his head, replied. "I don't speak Russian."

One of the officers challenged him. "What are you doing down here?" he said. "The parking lot is closed to the public for the moment."

"I'm sorry," Kang replied. He pointed. "My car is parked around the corner. I was just going to—"

"You'll have to come back for it later," the officer replied. "No vehicles are permitted to leave this facility until the emergency alarm has been turned off and this situation has been resolved."

"I understand," Kang said, then swung his weapon out from behind his leg and fired off two quick rounds. The bullets caught each officer in the leg. Kang watched them collapse to the ground. He walked up to them, squeezed off two more rounds, one to the head of each man, ending their lives, then set out in search of his quarry.

42

A Hard Right

MATT AND KYLA helped Soo, Tam, and Minho out of the transport cases while Rigor and Jules attended to Gran. Alexander Kurien double-clicked the Navigator's key fob. With a *chirp chirp* the vehicle's doors unlocked.

"Everybody good?" Matt asked.

Tam smiled. "That was cool! Minho liked it too!"

Matt tousled the boy's hair. "You guys did great," he replied. "Dr. Park?"

Soo nodded. "I'm fine." She turned to her mother. "You okay, Mom?"

"Don't worry about me, daughter," Gran replied. "I'm a lot less fragile than I look."

Rigor smiled. "You can say that again." He took Gran by her arm. "Mind if I help you into the car?"

Gran smiled. "If it's the back seat, absolutely!"

Jules helped Rigor lift Gran up and into the car, teased her. "I may have to keep my eye on you."

"Oh my," Gran replied. "Are you two together?"

Jules nodded. "We are."

Gran winked. "Just my luck."

Kurien helped Matt unload their weapons from the final case. The HALO jump equipment remained. "We don't have enough room in the Nav for this gear anymore. Not with three extra passengers."

"And a dog," Matt added.

Kurien nodded. "Yes, and a dog."

"Pull out the weapons and leave the jump gear," Matt said. "We don't have any further use for it anyway."

Rigor, Jules, and Kyla stepped to the back of the Nav. "Family's secure," Kyla said. "We're good to go."

From another section of the underground parking garage, the team heard a familiar sound. *Pop, pop... pop, pop.*

"That sounded like gunfire," Rigor said.

"Small arms," Jules added.

Kyla nodded. "One level up."

Matt clapped Kurien on his shoulder. "Time to roll."

Kurien threw open the door, jumped into the driver's seat. Matt took his place in the front passenger seat, while Rigor, Jules, and Kyla occupied the third row. For their safety, Soo and her family were seated in the second row.

Kurien pulled up to the VIP parking gate, waited for the barrier to read and accept the plate's diplomatic bar code. The gate rose quickly.

The Nav's tires squealed on the grippy parking garage floor as it rounded the corner to the first floor. Ahead lay the exit ramp leading to the surface.

Matt stared through the blacked out window as they reached the base of the ramp and waited for the steel exit door to rise. He reassured the Parks. "Stay calm. We'll be out of here soon."

"Guess I won't be needing this anymore," Jules said. She removed the cell phone Rigor had taken from the South Korean agent, lowered her window, tossed it out of the vehicle.

"Shit," Rigor said.

"What is it?" Matt asked.

"Coming around the corner," Rigor replied. "Sleepyhead is awake. And he looks pissed."

Kurien waited impatiently for the gate to clear the roof of the Navigator, then pulled the vehicle forward. A horrific squeak sounded throughout the garage as the bottom rail of the roll-up door scraped across the roof of the Nav.

"Someone's gonna need a paint job," Rigor said.

Thirty feet away, the sound of metal against metal stopped the foreign operative in his tracks. He stared at the SUV, then ran toward the vehicle as it cleared the gate, drove up the ramp, and reached the street.

Kurien made a hard right, hit the gas.

"Where are we going?" Matt asked.

"To the one place you can get out of Russia without being seen," Kurien replied.

"And that is?"

"My boat."

"We're going to need a better way to get out of here than a boat, Alexander," Matt replied.

Kurien smiled. "Don't be so sure about that."

Matt shook his head. "I hope you know what you're doing."

"Have I given you a reason not to trust me yet?"

"No."

"Exactly. And I'm not about to start now."

KANG RAN AS FAST as he could, tried unsuccessfully to catch up to the Navigator, picked up the discarded phone from the floor of the garage where it had been tossed from the vehicle, examined it.

His phone.

He pocketed it as he ran up the ramp, ducked under the rolling gate as it closed, made his way to the street, saw his fellow operative parked across the road. He ran to the car, jumped into the passenger seat, pointed, yelled. "They're in the black Navigator. Follow them!"

"Copy that," the agent replied.

He punched the gas.

Together they tore off after the fleeing SUV.

43

Probably Nothing

MATT GLANCED IN the Navigator's passenger-side mirror as Kurien exited Vladivostok's downtown core and traveled along the seaport drive. "Looks like we're clear," he said. "How much further?"

"Two minutes," Kurien replied. "My boat is located in a private marina next to the seaport. If you didn't know where to find it, you'd drive right past the entrance. It was designed that way. A ten-foot-high concrete wall keeps unwelcome visitors out and prying eyes from spying on the owners, many of whom are oligarchs or the region's most successful businessmen. The vessels docked in it are among the most luxurious yachts in all of eastern Russia."

"I've got a pretty nice boat back home too," Rigor said.

"Oh?" Kurien replied. "What kind? Benetti? Rossinavi? Broward?"

Rigor smiled. "Nah. She's a 1981 converted tugboat. 26 footer. Handles swells like a champ."

"A *tugboat?*" Kurien asked.

"Yep. I call her Annie."

"I see."

Jules chimed in. "Somehow I think Alexander's boat and Annie aren't even in the same class, Rig."

"Are you saying my boat isn't classy?" Rig retorted.

"Let me put it this way," Jules replied. "Your clients are once-a-year scuba divers and cigar-chomping fishing charter dudes whose idea of a pleasant day on the water is seeing who can chug the most beer then pee over the side the longest. So, classy? Not in the least."

Kurien smiled.

The traffic along the seawall was light; the afternoon sunny and bright.

"Looks like a good day to be out on the water," Matt said.

"Uh-huh," Kurien replied, his attention focused on his side mirror.

"What is it?" Matt asked.

"Probably nothing."

"Something caught your eye," Matt said.

Kurien nodded. "Behind us. A vehicle just rounded the corner. I think I recognize it."

"Meaning?"

"Before we left the city, an SUV just like it fell in behind us. I didn't think anything of it because it was so far back. Now, I'm not so sure."

"You think we're being followed?"

Kurien nodded. "Possibly."

Matt looked ahead. "Speed up. Take the next turn, then pull over."

"Why? We're almost at the marina."

"Do it."

Kurien accelerated down the road, took the corner, braked to a hard stop.

Matt opened his door, turned to Kyla. "If anything happens to me, leave. Get the family out of here. Got it?"

Kyla nodded.

Matt ran to the rear of the Navigator, dropped low, waited for the vehicle to come into view. He peered through the M18's scope, looked at the driver.

Unknown.

He swung the scope to the left, sighted the passenger.

Anwoo Kang.

"Son of a bitch," he said.

Matt took aim at the vehicle, opened up on the Chevy Tahoe's front grille, released a volley of rounds, watched as they found their mark behind the front grill. Smoke began to pour out from the engine compartment, obscured the driver's vision. Matt focused his next assault on the vehicle's front tires, took them out. One by one the tires exploded. The Tahoe swerved violently, first to the left, then the right. Finally, it left the road, jumped the curb, and crashed head-on into the concrete break wall. Matt watched as the passenger door opened. Kang fell out of the car, pushed himself to his feet, spied Matt, took aim, returned fire.

Matt retreated to his open door as Kang's rounds pinged off the ground at his feet. He jumped inside the vehicle, closed his door. "Go!"

Kurien punched the accelerator. The Navigator tore away from the curb, entered the road.

"Get us to the marina," Matt ordered. "Fast!"

44

No Witnesses

KANG SCREAMED OUT as he fired indiscriminately at the back of the fleeing vehicle, then checked on his partner. "Tran, you hit?"

Agent Tran pushed down the airbag, which had deployed when the Tahoe hit the break wall. "I'm good."

"Then get out," Kang demanded. He walked into the road, trained his weapon on an oncoming motorist, forced the car to stop, approached the driver, yanked open her door, dragged her from the car, threw her to the pavement. Staring up at Kang's gun, the panicked woman covered her face, begged for mercy. "Please don't hurt me," she cried. "I have a child!"

"Go!" Kang yelled.

The woman scrambled to her feet, ran across the road.

Pedestrians who had heard the gunfire and witnessed the ensuing crash ran to her and pulled her to safety. Together they hunkered down behind precast concrete flower beds.

Kang called out to his partner. "Tran! Move!"

Dazed from the impact, Agent Tran exited the Tahoe, shuffled to the stolen car, slid behind the wheel.

"Go!" Kang said.

Tran hit the gas. The Lada Vesta raced down the road.

In the distance, Kang watched the Navigator's brake lights flash. The car made a quick right turn.

"They're heading into the seaport," Tran said. "We've got them now."

Kang nodded. "When we find them, leave the big American for me."

"He's your unfinished business?"

"Fucking right he is."

"No problem."

"Just make sure Dr. Park isn't hurt."

"What about her family?"

"I don't give a damn about her family. She's the one we want. We kill everyone else. No witnesses."

Tran nodded. "Copy that."

45

Fortress 1

"COME ON, COME on, come on," Matt said impatiently as he waited for the beautiful wrought iron entrance gate leading into the marina to roll aside. When it was clear of the vehicle, Kurien hit the gas.

"Sorry, Reaper," Kurien said. "The gate was built for looks, not for speed. I should know. I ordered it." He followed the marina road around the corner, passed the clubhouse, and then stopped the Navigator behind the strangest-looking vessel Matt had ever seen.

The team and the family exited the Nav.

Rigor walked to the gangway, stared in amazement at the immense, magnificent craft, turned to Kurien. "What in the living hell is that?"

Kurien smiled. "That is *Fortress 1*. She's a MIGALOO M5

superyacht. Five hundred feet of nautical engineering mastery. Part luxury yacht, part submersible."

"So, it's a yacht *and* a submarine?"

"Correct."

"Holy shit!"

"I commissioned her to be built at the request of a small collective of my most important clients. They wanted a state-of-the-art vessel that could provide them and their families with the ultimate yachting experience as well as personal security, including protection against nuclear attack and electromagnetic pulse detonation should such catastrophes ever occur. Three years and two billion dollars later, here she sits. As her name implies, she is a fortress, both at sea and while docked."

Rigor whistled. "What's her range?"

"Nine thousand three hundred nautical miles. In the event of an emergency or attack while at sea, she can submerge to a depth of eight hundred feet and remain there for four weeks."

"Incredible," Rigor said.

Matt called out to his team. "Rig and Jules, help the family aboard and assist Alexander in getting the ship underway. Kyla and I will grab the weapons and bring them aboard."

"Copy that," Rigor said. He returned to the Navigator, helped Gran along the gangway to the boarding platform. Kurien opened the main cabin doors and began making the craft ready to leave the seaport.

Gran confided in Rigor. "I don't like boats," she said. "I don't do well on them. I get seasick very quickly."

Rigor helped her board the vessel. "Something tells me

this is going to be a very different experience for all of us. I'm sure you'll be okay."

"I hope so."

"I'll keep an eye on you."

"You promise?"

"Yes, ma'am. I promise."

"Thank you, Mr. Rigor."

Rigor smiled. "No *mister*, just Rig."

Gran nodded. "Okay, Rig."

Soo followed Tam and Minho aboard the super yacht, entered the main cabin. "Whoa," Tam said. "Mom, check this out!"

Fortress 1's interior appointments rivaled those of any of the world's most luxurious hotels, from brushed gold fixtures to opulently designed furnishings.

"It's incredible," Soo said.

"Incredible?" Tam replied. "It's more than just incredible. It's epic to the super duper max!"

Soo smiled. "Whatever you say."

Minho padded ahead, found a comfortable couch, jumped up, nestled into its velvety soft cushions, made himself at home.

Jules caught up with the family. "I'll check with Alexander and find out where he wants us to stay," she said.

"Thank you," Soo replied.

Matt and Kyla returned to the Navigator to retrieve their weapons. Matt stared at the marina entrance gate as it rolled closed at a lethargic pace. "That has to be the slowest gate in the world," he said. "So much for securi—"

Together they watched as a red Lada raced past the gate, locked up its brakes and squealed to a stop.

"What the hell?" Matt said.

The vehicle's engine whined as it backed up at speed, then turned and faced the closing gate.

Matt raised his assault rifle, sighted the car's passengers. "We have a problem," he said.

"Kang?" Kyla asked.

Matt nodded. "Yeah."

The driver hit the gas.

The very expensive wrought iron gate Kurien had gone to great pains to order for the marina was destroyed in an instant as Kang and his partner crashed the Lada through it.

As the vehicle bore down on the Navigator, Matt and Kyla came under fire.

46

Sometimes Things Get Messy

MATT YELLED OUT as the Lada braked to a stop and the South Korean operatives emerged from the damaged vehicle, guns firing. "Cover!"

Kyla ran from the Navigator, took a position behind a shipping container twenty feet away, watched as the driver trained his pistol on her, fired a shot.

The round ricocheted off the metal container, narrowly missed its mark.

Inside Fortress 1, Rigor and Jules heard the exchange of automatic weapons and small arms gunfire, then ran to the back of the superyacht. Jules rushed out onto the deck, only to be hit by the gunmen. The round tore through her shoulder. The sudden impact of the bullet spun her around and dropped her to the ground. She fell, striking her head on the deck.

Rigor watched her collapse, called out. "Julia!"

Kyla heard the cry, glanced over her shoulder, saw Rigor pick up Jules in his arms. "Get her inside!" Kyla yelled. "We've got this."

Rigor hurried Jules back into the yacht, called out. "Dr. Park!"

Soo turned to Tam. "Take your grandmother and Minho and go. Find somewhere to hide. I'll come for you when it's safe."

"But Mom!" Tam objected.

"Don't argue with me, Tam!" Soo yelled. "Do as I say! Move, all of you! *Now!*"

"I'll take care of them," Kurien said. He rushed into the large living room, removed his wallet from his pocket, pulled out a plastic card, touched it to the corner of an over-sized mirrored glass coffee table. The top of the table clicked open. He lifted the corner, raised the tabletop. Inside, the table was outfitted with a collection of weapons. He removed three guns and their accompanying magazines, inserted the mags, readied the weapons, handed one to Soo, the second to Gran. The final weapon he slipped into the small of his back. He addressed Soo and Gran.

"Have either of you ever shot a gun before?"

Soo and Gran nodded. "Mandatory military training," Soo replied. "Full disclosure... I'm a terrible shot."

"You don't need to be good," Kurien replied. "Just accurate. Look first. If the person is a threat, shoot. If they're not, don't shoot. Got it?"

Soo nodded.

"Don't I get a gun too?" Tam asked.

Kurien shook his head. "Not on your life, kid. Come with me."

Outside, the gunfire continued.

Rigor entered the living room as Kurien departed to safely hide Gran, Tam, and Minho. Jules lay slumped in his arms, unconscious. He spoke to Soo, his usual smart-alecky tone now gone. He sounded scared. "Gunshot wound to the left shoulder, doc," he said. "She's losing a lot of blood."

"Lay her on the couch," Soo said.

Rigor laid Jules down carefully on the large sofa and knelt beside her. Soo removed her jacket and shirt, inspected the site of the traumatic shoulder injury. "There's an exit wound," she said. "That's a good thing. I'll need to sterilize it and pack it as quickly as possible. Find me a first aid kit!"

Rigor jumped to his feet, looked around, spied a white metal box affixed to the wall clearly marked FIRST AID. He pulled the box off the wall, ran back to Soo, placed it on the coffee table in front of the couch, opened it. "How can I help?" he asked.

"Go to the galley," Soo ordered. "Grab as many towels as you can find. Soak them in hot water and bring them to me."

"Copy that."

Jules began to come around. She stirred at first, then tried to fight Soo as she bolted upright in a panic. "What happened?" she asked.

Soo spoke to her calmly, settled her. "It's all right," she said. "You've been shot."

"*Shot?*" Jules exclaimed. "What about Rigor? Is he…"

"Rigor is fine," Soo assured her. "He's in the galley helping me. He'll be back in a second."

"Matt and Kyla?"

"They're outside. We're under attack."

"The agents from the hotel?"

Soo nodded. "Has to be."

Jules tried to sit up. "I can't just lie here," she said. "Not when Matt and Kyla need help."

Rigor returned to the room. "You're not going anywhere," he said. He handed a hot towel to Soo.

Soo laid Jules back down on the couch. "This might sting a little," she said, then pressed the hot towel onto the wound.

Jules grimaced. "A little? *Damn!*"

Soo smiled. "Okay, maybe a lot." She removed the blood-soaked towel, examined the wound once more, tossed it aside, took a second towel from Rigor, applied it.

Rigor removed a bottle of antiseptic wash and a box of sterile gauze bandages from the first aid kit. "You want me to irrigate and pack it?" he asked.

Soo stared at him. "You've done this before?"

Rigor nodded. "Too many times. Unfortunately, when you're at war, sometimes things get messy."

Soo nodded. "Do it."

Rigor sighed. "Not gonna lie to you, babe. This is gonna hurt like a son of a bitch. You ready?"

Jules nodded. "Give me a sec to—"

Rigor squeezed the bottle, irrigated the wound generously with the antiseptic. The liquid bubbled as it seeped into the wound.

Jules screamed. "Holy hell! I told you to give me a second to prepare myself! What is the matter with you?"

"Think of it as the element of surprise," Rigor replied. "Worked, didn't it?"

"Do me a favor?"

"What?"

"Give me your gun."

"Why?"

"So I can shoot you! Don't worry, I'll extract the bullet... *with my teeth*."

Rigor cracked a smile. "Sweetheart, you sound upset."

"You think?"

Rigor looked at Soo, smiled. "She's going to be just fine."

Soo smiled. "I think so too." She helped lift up Jules to a seated position, spoke to Rigor. "Hand me a few rolls of gauze. I'll wrap her shoulder."

"You've got it," Rigor said. "You need me for anything else, doc?"

Soo shook her head. "No. Jules will be fine. She'll be in a lot of pain for a while, but fine nonetheless."

Rigor stood. "I have to find Matt and Kyla." He bent down, kissed Jules's forehead. "I'll be back," he said.

Jules nodded. "You better be, you big lump."

Rigor smiled, ran to the rear of the yacht, picked up one of the M18 assault rifles Matt had brought from the Navigator, took cover, scanned the area.

The gunshots had stopped.

Matt and Kyla were nowhere to be seen.

A small car sat in the marina parking lot well back from the Navigator, its engine compartment hissing, steam rising from its demolished front end, both driver and passenger doors open, absent of occupants or bodies.

Rigor raised his assault rifle. Front sight focused, he left the safety of Fortress 1 and hurried down the gangway in search of his teammates.

47

Mr. Close-Quarters Combat

ATT SPIED KYLA standing at the rear of the large seafaring shipping container, rifle in hand, raised and ready, waiting for the gunman who had just tried to kill her to make himself known. He rapped his knuckles on the hood of the Navigator.

Kyla glanced over her shoulder, saw him.

Matt touched his chest, then motioned with his hand to indicate the direction in which he would be moving from his present position. Left. He pointed to Kyla, indicated the direction he wanted her to go. Right.

Kyla understood. Matt wanted them to circle the grounds, find and eliminate the threat. She nodded, followed her rifle sight as she walked alongside the container, paused before she reached its corner, took a deep breath, let it out, then peered out at the abandoned car.

The gunman's second round came just as close to her as his first. It whizzed over her head, missed her by inches. She ducked back behind the container, called out. "Two chances to kill me and you missed both times. Don't they teach you how to shoot at NIS spy school?"

Tran waited, listened, zoned in on the location of Kyla's voice. Behind the shipping container. He moved from his position behind the Lada, ran a short distance across the marina, found cover behind the base of a ship-to-shore crane, crept around the machine, searched for the American operative. At last, he found himself with a perfect view of the container.

The woman was gone.

Tran swore to himself, left the protective cover of the crane, ran to the base of a large ballast keel undergoing repairs, dropped to one knee, sought to reacquire his target.

"Looking for me?" Kyla said.

The voice came from behind him.

"Lose the weapon," Kyla ordered.

Tran dropped his pistol on the ground, raised his hands, stood. "You're quick," he said. "How did you get here so fast?"

"I excelled at track and field," Kyla replied. "You know the drill. On your knees, hands behind your head, cross your feet."

"You're arresting me?" Tran asked. "I didn't think the CIA went in for that sort of thing."

"We don't. I'd just feel better knowing—"

Tran made his move, withdrew the knife he had secured in a sheath behind his back, threw it at Kyla with all his might, then jumped to his feet and ran at her, closing the gap between them as the razor-sharp blade sliced through the air.

Kyla turned her body away from the deadly weapon as it rushed toward her, felt an explosion of white-hot pain as the blade grazed her forearm and caused her to drop her assault rifle.

Tran was on her in seconds. He yelled as he took to the air and thrust out his leg, the flying side kick finding its mark, crushing Kyla's wounded arm against her body, sending her reeling backwards, her back slamming against the steel ballast keel. A shock wave of pain racked her body, dropped her to her knees. Darkness clouded her vision. She fought to recover from the powerful assault as she pulled herself to her feet.

"It seems what I lack in shooting skills I make up for in close-quarters combat," Tran said. He picked the throwing knife up off the ground, then began walking towards Kyla.

Kyla looked over her shoulder, saw she had no obstructions behind her, put some distance between her and the South Korean assassin. She nodded. "I've got to hand it to you. The knife holstered behind the back was good. I never saw that one coming." She brought her hand to her right ear, unclipped her earring, opened it with her fingers, lowered her hand to her side.

Tran smiled. "This will be a first for me," he said.

"What will be?" Kyla asked.

"Killing a CIA operative. Even better that you're a woman."

"That makes a difference?" Kyla asked. "How many extra points does that get you?"

Tran shook his head. "No extra points. I've just always thought it would be more... *fun*."

"I'm sure for you it'll be a barrel of laughs," Kyla replied. "For me? Not so much."

"That's kind of the idea."

"Of course, using a knife doesn't exactly make this a clean kill for you, does it?"

"Meaning?"

"Wouldn't you prefer to take me out the old-fashioned way with your hands. Besides, you're Mr. Close-Quarters Combat, right?"

Tran nodded. "You're right." He tossed the knife on the ground between them. "Tell you what. I'll make this interesting. If you get to the knife first, you'll have the advantage. Do your worst with it. But if I get to it first, I'll gut you like a deer. Deal?"

Kyla shrugged. "Doesn't sound like I have much of a choice."

Tran shook his head. "You don't."

Kyla sighed. "That's what I thought you'd say." She leaned forward, positioned herself as though she was about to make a run for the knife.

Tran moved first, ran for the weapon.

Kyla struck out in a flash, threw her double-bladed earring at Tran. The throwing star found its mark in the operative's throat.

Tran clutched at his neck, tried to remove the blood-drenched weapon that had taken him completely by surprise and embedded itself in his larynx, couldn't. He fell to his knees, stared up at Kyla.

Kyla retrieved her rifle from the ground, closed the

distance between them, picked up Tran's knife, spoke to the agent. "Hurts, doesn't it?"

Tran looked into her eyes; his words impossible to understand as he attempted to reply. Gurgling sounds emanated from his throat. Kyla leaned over, put her ear to his mouth. "What's that?" she asked. "I can keep the knife? Thanks. Don't mind if I do. Besides, you won't be needing it anymore... what with you dying and all."

Tran fought to breathe, clawed at his throat, made two more feeble attempts to remove the modified throwing star. Finally, he dropped his head. His arm fell limply at his side.

Kyla waited until the agent took his final breath and watched him die. She pocketed his pistol and his knife, spoke aloud. "One asshole down, one to go."

She picked up her weapon and hurried off in search of Matt.

48

Broken

MATT CREPT THROUGH the marina in search of Anwoo Kang. The South Korean operative had run from his position behind the disabled Lada after his partner fired the shot which had taken down Jules. "You're not going anywhere, Kang," he called out. "Might as well make it easy on yourself. Step out. I promise I won't kill you."

No reply.

Matt investigated the wet slips, pilings, and piers near Fortress 1, found no sign of the NIS operative. He glanced over his shoulder, watched Rigor move quickly along the gangway, then drop low and out of sight.

Across the yard, chains rattled.

Matt moved from one cover position to the next and

stopped behind a neatly organized coil of heavy rope mooring lines, peered around them.

The tremendous blow took him by surprise. The chain came out of nowhere, whipped around the stack of mooring lines, and caught him squarely in the face. Matt fell back, felt the bite of the links as they ripped into his skin and opened a gash under his eye. He raised his hand to his cheek, felt the sticky ooze of his blood as it poured out from the deep wound.

Kang stepped around the stack of ropes, the length of heavy chain swinging loosely in his hand. He raised his pistol, leveled it at Matt. "What was that you said about making it easy?"

His vision compromised by the vicious assault, Matt's left eye watered. Soon it would be swollen shut, leaving him nearly defenseless against Kang. He pushed himself to his feet. His assault rifle lay on the ground, out of reach. He stared at the weapon, calculated his next move.

Kang circled Matt, staying in the region of his now blind left peripheral vision, his weapon trained on him. He swung the chain, taunted him. "Where's the big guy?" he asked.

Matt turned in step with Kang, fought to keep him in sight. "Big guy?"

Kang nodded. "The guy who choked me out. Where is he?"

Matt shrugged. "Beats me. Why?"

"Because if it's not too much trouble, I'd really like to put a bullet in his head. You mind calling out and asking him to join the party?"

Matt shook his head. "I'd rather not."

"That was a demand, not a request."

"Too bad I don't take demands from you."

Kang smiled, draped the chain around his neck. He removed his cell phone, placed a call, spoke briefly, then hung up.

"You really fucked up your car when you crashed the gate," Matt asked. "You calling for an Uber?"

Kang smiled. "No."

"Skip the Dishes? DoorDash?"

Kang chuckled. "I'm impressed that you're able to maintain a sense of humor under these circumstances."

Matt shrugged. "What can I say? It's a gift."

"Good. Because life is about to get a lot less funny for you."

"How's that?"

"That call I just made was for backup. Ten minutes from now, this marina will be flooded with my men."

"Too bad. I was hoping we'd be able to keep this little party to ourselves."

"Fine by me," Kang replied. "We could have a little fun until my men arrive."

"What did you have in mind?"

"I could beat the hell out of you while you try to beat the hell out of me."

"*Try?*" Matt replied.

"Trust me, it's no contest."

"Cocky little prick, aren't you?"

"Very. You ready?"

"You see me going anywhere?"

Kang smiled. "Look at you. Broken... bleeding... half-blind. How pathetic. If you're any example of the best operative your country has to offer, one thing is for certain."

"What's that?"

"America is fucked."

Matt brought his hand to his face, wiped away the blood as it gushed from the wound, forced a smile. "I wouldn't be so sure about that."

Kang slipped his pistol into the small of his back, removed the chain from around his neck, swung it in a tight circle at his side. "I'm going to enjoy this."

"Last chance," Matt said. "Live or die. Your choice."

Kang lashed out with the chain, caught Matt once more on his face. The explosion of pain spun Matt around. The second attack opened the wound even more. He cried out from the pain, brought his hand to his face, touched his now exposed cheekbone. He wouldn't be able to take one more blow from the chain. Of that he was certain. He would be rendered unconscious, then Kang would surely kill him.

Behind Kang, a voice called out.

"Hey, shithead," Rigor said. "Remember me?"

Kang turned.

Twenty feet away stood Rigor and Kyla, their weapons trained on the South Korean operative.

Kyla spoke. "In case you were wondering, your partner is dead. And I'm happy to report, he died slowly and painfully, like you're about to now."

Kang smiled. "I'm not surprised. He wasn't my first choice for backup. What can you do? Sometimes you just have to work with what you've got."

"You okay, Matt?" Rigor asked.

Matt turned to his right, stared at Rigor through his good eye. "Fine. Cocky Little Prick and I were just chatting."

"Looks like you were doing more than chatting," Rigor replied.

Matt waved his hand, shook his head. "Do us a favor?"

"What?"

"Give me a minute with this asshole. This won't take long."

Kang turned back to Matt. "Now who's the cocky little pri—"

Matt rushed forward, closed the gap between them, thrust the heels of his palms under Kang's ribs, then followed through with a crushing hammer fist deep into the operative's solar plexus. Kang felt his sternum shatter and the air leave his lungs. He stood for a moment, mouth ajar, his mind communicating to his body just how severe the attack had been, as though Matt's fist had traveled not just through his chest but out his back.

Matt stepped forward, relieved the operative of the chain he held in his hand, tossed it aside.

Kang fell to his knees.

Matt slipped his hand behind his back, withdrew one of the ceramic knives he had kept hidden in his waistband, stared down at Kang. "Like I said, cocky little prick." He drove the blade deep into Kang's left eye, twisted it sharply, then pulled it out, wiped it clean on the man's tuxedo jacket. "Hurts like hell, doesn't it?" he said. He picked up his assault rifle, slung it over his shoulder, turned, walked towards Rigor and Kyla.

Kyla lowered her rifle. "You done now?"

Matt stopped. "No," he answered. "As a matter of fact, I'm not."

He walked back to Kang, removed the dual-purpose auto injector/IED pen from inside his jacket pocket, discarded its purple end cap, rammed the pen deep into Kang's eye socket, then yelled over his shoulder. "Get to the ship. Run!"

Rigor and Kyla turned and ran.

Matt grabbed Kang by his lapels, pulled him up, stared into his dying eyes. "This is for Julia," he said. He twisted the purple collar on the improvised explosive device, then ran around the stacks of coiled rope after his teammates.

Seconds later, the RX-27 blast gel within the pen exploded.

Kang's head left his lifeless body. His torso fell forward.

The three operatives hurried back to Fortress 1, boarded the superyacht.

"That was a little extreme, wasn't it?" Rigor asked.

Matt pointed to his cheek. "You see what he did to my face?"

Rigor winced. "Looks nasty. You're going to need a Band-Aid."

"Just one?"

"Okay, maybe a stitch or three. Lucky for you we have a first aid kit on board and a doctor who is trained to do just that."

Kyla handed Matt a towel she had soaked in cold water. "Press this against the wound," she said. "It'll reduce the swelling until Dr. Park can sew you up."

Matt took the towel, nodded. "Thanks." He looked around. "Where is everybody?"

"We're here," Alexander Kurien called out as he walked around the corner accompanied by Soo, Gran, Tam, Jules, and Minho.

Matt saw they were armed. "Hang onto those weapons until we get out of here." He turned to Kyla, Rigor, Jules, and Kurien. "Kang made a call. His men will be here any minute. How fast can you get us out of here, Alexander?"

"Immediately."

Matt nodded. "Go."

Kurien ran to the captain's station, engaged Fortress 1's mighty engines.

The team and family steadied themselves as the submersible superyacht pulled away from its berth and headed out of the Port of Vladivostok.

The team stared out from the ship's sealed stern doors and watched as armed agents converged upon the marina, left their cars, then spread out in search of the escaped American operatives and the high-value asset they would never find.

Fortress 1 cleared the port, entered the Sea of Japan.

Matt joined Kurien at the helm. "Where to?" Kurien asked. "We have the sea all to ourselves."

"Where are your maps?" Matt asked.

Kurien pointed to a waist-high rectangular table behind him the size of a large flat-screen television. "It's a Smartmap," he said. "Touch the surface and search. It'll chart a course for us anywhere in the world you want to go."

Matt activated the screen, found his desired destination. "Take us around the southern tip of South Korea, then north up the coast to Pyeongtaek." He provided Kurien with the required GPS coordinates.

Kurien tapped the superyacht's control panel. "Course plotted. We're on autopilot now."

"How long will it take to get there?" Matt asked.

Kurien checked the ship's digital display. "That's a distance of two hundred and ninety nautical miles," he replied. "Our speed when submerged is twelve knots. That makes twenty-four hours, give or take a few minutes.

"Good," Matt said. "I'll tell everyone to get some rest."

Kurien smiled. "Not before they witness the magic."

"Magic?"

Kurien nodded. "Call everyone to the windows. They won't want to miss this."

Matt complied with Kurien's request.

The group stood at the windows and watched in amazement as Fortress 1 submerged beneath the calm water of the Sea of Japan.

49

Hard Enough

MATT KNOCKED LIGHTLY on the door to the stateroom Kurien had assigned to Jules and Rigor.

Rigor answered the door, opened it quietly, stepped out into the corridor, eased the door closed behind him. "Hey, Matt," he whispered. "Everything okay?"

Matt nodded. "Fine. I thought I'd check in on Jules. How's she doing?"

"She's sleeping now. Took a while, though. She'd come down with a wicked fever. It just broke. Completely soaked the sheets. Doc said that was to be expected under the circumstances. How about you? You haven't had your cheek checked out yet?"

"I'm on my way to the medical bay now. Dr. Park is waiting for me."

Rigor examined the cut. "Swelling's going down. The eye doesn't look so bad now, but your cheek looks like crap."

Matt smiled. "I'll be back to adorning the covers of GQ before you know it."

"Thanks for the visual," Rigor replied. "I'm never going to get that scary thought out of my mind."

"Modeling's a lot safer than what we do."

"Yeah, but not nearly as much fun," Rigor replied. "When was the last time you heard of a male model taking out a couple of South Korean assassins?"

"Not recently."

"I rest my case."

"How about you, Rig? You good?"

Rigor winked. "Buddy, I was just getting warmed up. What about Kyla? How's her wing?"

"The knife glanced off her forearm. No stitches required."

"That's good. All things considered, I'd say we got off lucky."

Matt nodded. "We did."

Inside the cabin, Jules stirred.

"I'd better go back inside and keep an eye on her," Rigor said.

Matt nodded. "We've got a few hours to kill until we reach our destination. Get some rest. You've earned it."

Rigor opened the door, entered the room, turned. "Right back at ya, pal."

MATT MADE his way to Fortress 1's fully equipped medical bay where Soo was waiting. "Here he is," she said as he entered the room. "My last patient of the day. How are you feeling?"

"Like I've been hit in the face with a chain. Twice."

Soo bit her lip, stifled a smile. "It didn't occur to you to duck?"

Matt forced a smile. "Guess I'm a slow learner."

Soo pulled a steel medical cart up beside her and patted the examination table with her hand. "Hop up."

Matt sat on the table.

"Tilt your head back."

Tam sat on a stool in the corner of the room, watching his mother work. Minho lay on the floor, snoring lightly.

Matt winced as Soo examined his wound.

"Does it hurt?" Tam asked.

Matt glanced at the boy out of the corner of his good eye. "A little. Not too much."

"A bad guy did that to you, huh?"

"Yeah."

"Did you hit him back? Mom says it's okay to hit someone back if they hit you first."

"Your mom is right. And yes, I hit him back."

"Hard?"

"Hard enough."

"Did you knock him out?"

Matt recalled driving his ceramic knife deep into Kang's eye socket, twisting the blade, pulling it out, ramming the explosive IED injector pen into the impaled cavity, setting the detonator, then escaping before the explosion came five seconds later which blew the head off the foreign operative and ended his life. "You could say that," he replied.

"Enough talk of violence, Tam," Soo warned as she stitched up the gash on Matt's cheek. "The men who were after us were very bad people. They wanted to hurt us. Matt's injury is the result of the action he took to save our lives and his own. We owe him everything."

"Not everything, Doc. I'll settle for the Synoxin-9 formula and its accompanying research."

Soo nodded. "I'll provide you with everything your government will need to know about the formula as soon as we're reunited with my brother."

"That won't be a problem. You'll see him shortly."

"When we arrive?"

Matt nodded. "I'll set the wheels in motion as soon as we're done here."

"Thank you," Soo said.

"You're welcome."

TFC Cross took Matt's call. "Reaper," he said. "Sitrep."

"We're good, sir. We have Dr. Park, her family, and the Synoxin-9 research."

"Did you say her *family*?"

"Yes, sir. It's a long story."

"Where are you now?"

"En route to South Korea's northwest coast. We should be there within twenty-four hours. Your friend, Alexander Kurien, came through for us big time. We're aboard his submarine in the Sea of Japan."

"Kurien has a submarine?"

"It's a hybrid luxury yacht and submersible. Her name is Fortress 1."

"Well, I'll be damned."

"We have a problem though, sir."

"What kind of problem?"

"As it turns out, it wasn't the Russians we had to worry about. It was South Korea."

"What do you mean?"

"We ran into a team of National Intelligence Service operatives. They were there for Dr. Park just like we were."

"And?"

"We handled it."

"And the Parks?"

"Unharmed, sir. But now that we're aware South Korea is also after Synoxin-9, we'll need protection."

"What's your destination?"

"The Pyeongtaek seaport. It's the closest we can get to US Army Garrison Humphreys. My concern is that the South Koreans might try to stop us, even attempt to board us and kidnap Dr. Park."

"Are they aware she's on board?"

"No, sir. But we weren't aware that they were a threat until today. Knowing they are, I'd appreciate it if you'd make a call on our behalf."

"To?"

"Busan Naval Base. Tell them we're transporting a high-value intelligence asset who is in our custody. Ask them to dispatch an American destroyer to our coordinates and escort us to Pyeongtaek. But this has to be done quietly. The Korean Navy is also stationed at Busan. They can't be made aware of what's going on. It could incite an incident that neither of our countries want."

"I'll make the call right now."

"Thank you, sir. Just one last thing."

"Name it."

"Dr. Park's brother needs to be transferred from holding

at our black site to Army Garrison Humphreys. Reuniting him with his family was part of the deal. We need to honor it."

"He'll be there when you arrive. You have my word."

"Thank you, sir."

"Good work, Matt. Extend my thanks to your team."

"I will, sir."

"Give me your GPS coordinates. I'll have an escort ship sent to you immediately."

"Copy that, sir."

50

Gone But Never Forgotten

NORTHWEST OF THE island city of Tsushima, Japan, Kurien heard the call over Fortress 1's ship-to-shore communications system. "This is the U.S. Navy destroyer USS Arcadia hailing the vessel Fortress 1. Do you read? Over."

Kurien replied. "USS Arcadia, this is the recreational submersible Fortress 1. Responding to your call. Over."

The commander spoke. "Fortress 1, this is Commander Alan Goodson speaking. Abort your dive and ascend to the surface. We have orders to escort you from your current location to Pyeongtaek. Acknowledge. Over."

"USS Arcadia, Fortress 1. Acknowledged. Be advised we are preparing to surface. Releasing our marker beacon now."

"Roger that," Goodson replied. From the Arcadia's

bridge he scanned the water with his binoculars, searched for the location beacon, saw it break the surface. Its strobe light began to flash. "We have you, Fortress 1. You're clear to surface."

"Roger that," Kurien replied.

Matt and Kyla joined Kurien at Fortress 1's bridge. "We must be ascending," Matt said.

"We are," Kurien said. "The escort you requested is waiting for us topside."

That was fast, Matt thought. It seemed Task Force Chief Cross's request for assistance had reached the highest levels of Naval command in no time.

Rigor and Jules entered the bridge. "What a weird feeling," Jules said. "I thought I was floating, then I realized we were ascending."

"Same here," Rigor said. "Very cool."

As Fortress 1 broke the surface, Commander Goodson hailed the vessel once again. "We have you directly ahead of us, Fortress 1. Stay on your present course. We'll be right behind you all the way."

Kurien replied. "Thanks for having our back, Arcadia."

"Our pleasure. Arcadia out."

THE USS ARCADIA followed Fortress 1 past Jeju-do Island, South Korea's southernmost point, around the tip of the country at Jeollanam-Do, north through the Yellow Sea, around Elephant Rock, and through the Gyeonggi-do Passage.

Commander Goodson hailed the superyacht. "Fortress 1, acknowledge."

Kurien replied. "Fortress 1."

"Looks like this is as far as we go," Goodson said. "There are two impassable seawalls ahead. Not to worry. We have transportation inbound via helo. Prepare to be boarded."

"Understood, Arcadia," Kurien replied. "Advise your incoming helo we are equipped with a touch-and-go helipad on our aft deck. Ready to receive you."

"Roger that," Goodson replied. "By the way, Captain. That looks like one hell of a ship you've got there."

"She is, sir," Kurien said. "You're welcome to come aboard if you'd like. I'll be happy to give you the nickel tour."

"Thanks for the offer, Fortress 1, but we've made other plans for the day."

Kurien keyed his mic, laughed. "I'm sure you have, Commander."

Matt and Kyla opened the rear doors of the cabin, felt the incoming rush of warm air as it blew through the ship. In the distance could be heard the mighty thrum of the inbound helicopter's powerful rotors.

"Our ride's almost here," Matt said. "Kyla, get the Park's. Tell Tam he's going to love this."

Kyla smiled. "Copy that."

The family appeared on the bridge a minute later, belongings in hand. Frightened by the roar of the helicopter, Minho ran back inside. Tam chased after him, returned with the dog at his side, securely leashed.

Tam called out to his mother above the roar of the SH-60 Seahawk as it touched down on Fortress 1's helipad. "Check it out, Mom! A real-life army helicopter!"

"Yes, it is," Soo replied.

Tam turned to Matt. "Is that for us?"

Matt nodded. "It is."

"Where are we going?"

"United States Army Garrison Humphreys. You and your family will be safe there."

"Is everyone coming?"

Matt looked at Tam, teased the boy. "You think we'd miss going for a ride with you in a helicopter as cool as that?"

Tam smiled. "No."

"Exactly. Come on. I'll get you and Minho on board first."

"Cool!"

Matt picked up Minho, held him in one arm, took Tam's hand, walked him to the chopper, loaded both boy and dog on board. "Hold on tight to Minho," Matt said. "He's still not sure what to make of this. He'll settle down in a minute."

"Copy that," Tam said officially.

Matt chuckled at the boy's response, then returned to his team, Soo, and Gran. "You guys are up next," he said. "Rigor, Jules, give Dr. Park and her mother a hand. Kyla and I will grab the gear."

"Copy that," Rigor said. He held out his arm for Gran. "May I escort you to the helicopter, young lady?" he asked.

Gran took Rigor's big arm in hers, squeezed his firm bicep, smiled. "You can escort me anywhere, handsome!"

Rigor laughed as they walked arm-in-arm to the Seahawk. "You don't quit, do you?"

Gran shook her head. "Never."

Soo picked up her computer bag, slung it over her shoulder. She talked with Jules as they walked to the chopper. "It's hard to imagine, isn't it?" Soo said.

"What is?"

"The extent to which one country will go to dominate another."

"Or the world."

Soo shook her head. "This madness has to stop."

Jules nodded. "From your lips to God's ears, Doctor."

The women reached the aircraft, climbed aboard, took their seats.

Matt and Kyla collected their weapons, stored them aboard the chopper. "Wait here," Matt said. "Tell the pilot I'll be ready to leave in a minute."

Kyla nodded. "Copy that."

Matt walked to the cabin door where Kurien stood watching the family and team board the aircraft. "So," Matt said. "I guess this is goodbye."

Kurien nodded. "I guess it is."

Matt extended his hand. "The American government owes you a debt of gratitude, Alexander. I can't thank you enough for everything you've done to help me, my team, and TFC Cross."

Kurien smiled, shook Matt's hand. "Don't mention it. Although you could tell Cameron he owes me a new Lincoln Navigator. I'm pretty sure that by now the South Korean government has towed mine from the marina and impounded it."

Matt nodded. "I'll make sure the CIA picks up the tab for your ride. So, where to from here?"

Kurien sighed. "I'm not sure. I hear there's great scuba diving off the Sapporo reef. Never been. Maybe I'll head up the coast of Japan and check it out for myself."

"Sounds like one hell of a trip."

"Then again, I could find myself a nice scenic setting somewhere underwater and just hang out there for a week or two. There's something about watching a movie in Fortress 1's theatre when you're two hundred feet below the surface that never gets old."

Matt smiled. "Sounds like a plan without a plan."

Kurien nodded. "Aren't those the best kind?"

"They are."

Kurien pointed to the chopper. "You better get going, Reaper. That thing costs a fortune to operate and you're burning fuel talking to me."

Matt smiled. "Uncle Sam is footing the bill, not me. Take care, Alexander. Thanks again."

"Forget it," Kurien replied. "It was fun."

Matt turned, walked to the Seahawk, climbed aboard.

Kurien watched the helicopter lift off Fortress 1's helipad, take to the air, then bank hard to the right en route to Camp Humphreys.

As the USS Arcadia executed her turn in the seaport to return to Busan, Kurien sealed Fortress 1's cabin doors, turned on the ship's music system, turned up Springsteen's *Born in the U.S.A*, and set a course for Sapporo.

He would miss his newfound friends.

They would be gone but never forgotten.

51

First Things First

THE SEAHAWK TOUCHED down on the tarmac at United States Army Garrison Humphreys in Pyeongtaek, South Korea. The team and the family disembarked the chopper, hurried to three waiting military police Jeeps. Together they drove to the administrative building where they were greeted by base Commander Eric Leavens. "Welcome to USAG Humphreys," Leavens said. "Which one of you is Reaper?"

Matt stepped forward. "That would be me, sir."

Leavens shook Matt's hand.

"This is my team," Matt continued. "And our very special guests, Dr. Soo Park of North Korea's NEST 5, and her family."

Leavens smiled. "It's a pleasure to meet you all. Dr. Park, I believe you have something for us?"

Soo smiled, patted her computer bag with her hand. "I do, Commander. But first things first."

"Understood," Leavens replied. "Follow me."

The team and the family accompanied the commander into the building and to the main boardroom. "Please take a seat," Leavens said.

"Thank you, Commander," Soo replied. "But I'm too nervous to sit."

Matt walked behind Soo, put his hand on her shoulder. "It's all right, Doctor," he said. "We've got you."

Leavens smiled. He pressed a button on the triangular speaker located in the middle of the table, spoke. "Send him in."

Muted voices in the hallway. Americans, save for one familiar voice.

Soo brought her hands to her mouth as her brother walked into the boardroom. "Hyon!" she cried, then ran into his arms.

Hyon Bak, who had trusted his life to the Sea of Japan and successfully escaped his communist country, hugged Soo, his mother, and his young nephew.

Minho whined, nudged his way in between the foursome.

Tam teased his dog. "You always have to be the center of attention, don't you?"

Minho looked up at his master, wagged his tail, panted happily.

Soo stepped away from her brother, took Matt's hand in hers. "I can't thank you enough for all you and your team have done to help my family." She handed Matt her computer bag. "Everything your government needs to know about Synoxin-9 is on this laptop. I'll be happy to meet with your experts to break down the formula and explain its mechanism of action."

"Thank you, Dr. Park. I'm sure that will be required."

Soo nodded. "There's one more thing about Synoxin-9 that you should know."

"What's that?" Matt asked.

"When your people examine the formula's chemical structure, they'll find it to be inert. In layman's terms, it won't work as presented."

Matt was confused. "Are you saying the formula for Synoxin-9 is a fake?"

Soo shook her head. "Not at all. Synoxin-9 is very real and very deadly. But I intentionally omitted a chemical branch agent. I'm the only one who knows what that agent is and where it fits in the molecular chain."

"And you'll provide us with that missing agent?"

"I will."

"What about the data you uploaded to the NEST 5 servers? Is that not accurate?"

"As far as my former government knows, it is. Is it harmful in its present form? Yes, but to a minimal degree. Will it kill? No. The formula I provided to the Reconnaissance General Bureau will mimic the effects of Synoxin-9, but it is not much more than a chemical irritant. If deployed, those affected will experience a cough, sore throat, and runny eyes, but nothing more. Unlike the real formula for Synoxin-9, it is not a weapon of mass destruction, nor can it be intelligently controlled when released into the air. I never want to see it used for such a purpose."

"Nor is that the intention of the US government," Matt replied. "Unlike North Korea, Egypt and South Sudan, America has signed the Chemical Weapons Convention. My expectation is that once you have explained to our people everything that we need to know about Synoxin-9 it will disappear. The formula will be transferred to a secret facility co-managed by the National Security Agency and the Centers for Disease Control and Prevention's Laboratory Response Network for Chemical Threats. It will never see the light of day."

Soo smiled. "That's exactly what I was hoping for."

"I have it on good authority that your family will be relocated to Colorado, which is exactly what Hyon wanted," Matt said. "It was a condition of his cooperation."

"He's talked about Colorado for as long as I can remember. It's the only place he's ever wanted to live."

"What about you?"

"I'll be happy wherever your government places us as long as we remain together."

Matt smiled. "You can't ask for more than that."

Soo smiled, shook her head. "No, you can't."

Commander Leavens approached Soo and Matt. "Dr. Park, my team would like to meet with you first thing in the morning after you and your family have had a good night's sleep. We'd like you to walk us through the science behind Synoxin-9."

"Of course, Commander," Soo replied. "It would be my pleasure."

"Very well," Leavens said. "If you'll excuse me, I have other matters to attend to."

"Thank you, Commander," Matt said.

Leavens nodded. "Don't mention it. We're always happy to help out our friends at the Agency."

.   .   .

RIGOR WALKED UP TO TAM, tousled his hair. "Hey, pal," he said. "Pretty cool helicopter ride, huh?"

Tam nodded. "The coolest!"

"You hungry?"

"Starving."

"Jules and I are going to the commissary to grab a bite to eat. You want to come along? Gran will be joining us too." He leaned over, whispered in the boy's ear. "She won't let me out of her sight!"

Tam smiled. "Sounds great!"

"What are you in the mood for? Popeye's? Subway? Taco Bell?"

"I don't know what those are," Tam replied. "What's a Taco Bell?"

Rigor opened his mouth, feigned a look of surprise. "*What's a Taco Bell?* Buddy, you haven't lived until you've had Taco Bell." He put his arm around the boy as they walked together. "Crunchy taco shell, warm beef filling, secret recipe taco sauce, lettuce, onion, tomato... it's pure gastronomical artistry."

"Gastro*what*?"

"It tastes frickin' awesome."

Tam smiled. "Cool!"

Rigor called out. "Come on, guys. Little Man here needs a taco fix. Commissary. Let's go!"

Minho chuffed.

Rigor scratched the dog's head. "Yes, Minho. You can come too."

Tam talked with Rigor as they walked to the commissary. "Know what's a drag?" he said.

"What's that, pal?"

"I was supposed to speak at the conference. I was really looking forward to it."

"Want to know something?" Rigor said.

"Sure."

"I don't think that crowd was smart enough to listen to you and your mom. They wouldn't have understood what you had to say."

"You think so?"

"Absolutely! You guys are *way* smarter than they could ever be. What's more, when you get to the States, you'll have the chance to meet people who are as bright as you are. I'd say brighter, but from what I hear you're a genius."

"So they say."

"Just remember one thing."

"What?"

"Being a genius is awesome, but don't forget to be a kid, too."

Tam smiled. "I won't."

"Good," Rigor said. They reached the Taco Bell counter. "Now, are you ready to have your taste buds blown?"

Tam smiled. "You bet!"

"All right, kiddo. Here we go. Welcome to America!"

EPILOGUE

ICOE

THE C-130 HERCULES military aircraft taxied along the tarmac at South Korea's Incheon Airport. Matt, Kyla, Rigor, and Jules relaxed in their seats as the plane lifted off and took to the sky, weary after the stress and strain of their first successful mission as a new team. The free lift home came compliments of Commander Leavens.

"How are you feeling, Jules?" Matt asked.

Jules massaged her wounded shoulder. "I won't lie. It hurts like a bitch."

Matt nodded. "Getting shot tends to have that effect on people."

"It's my own damn fault," Jules said. "I should have been on my toes, and I wasn't. I heard the car crash through the gate, knew you and Kyla were at the Navigator retrieving our gear and weapons. By the time I realized the danger you both were in, I'd been hit. Sorry, Matt. I'll make sure that never happens again."

"Don't worry about it," Matt replied. "The main thing is we didn't lose you. That would have been real bad. Especially for Rig."

"For me?" Rigor asked.

"Yeah. If Jules had been taken out, Soo's mother would be walking you down the aisle right about now."

Jules and Kyla laughed.

Rigor smiled. "What can I say? Women of all ages find me irresistible."

Jules nodded. "Sorry to say, but Rig's right. You should see them hanging around the dive shop, like pilot fish around a shark."

"Speaking of sharks," Kyla said. "I have a request."

"What's that?" Jules asked.

"I've always wanted to go deep sea fishing. Think you can hook me up... pardon the pun?"

"Absolutely," Rigor replied. "I know all the best spots. Bluefin, barracuda, snapper... you name the catch, I know where to fish for it."

"That sounds fantastic," Kyla replied. "Can we let Matt come too?"

Rigor winked. "If we must."

Matt chuckled. "Gee, thanks."

"I don't know about you guys," Jules said, "but I'm taking the next few days off. I need to give the shoulder time to heal. The best way I know how to do that is to spend the day at the beach, reading a book and sipping piña coladas until the sun sets over Carlisle Bay."

"I'll be happy to join you," Kyla offered.

GARY WINSTON BROWN

"Two's a party," Jules said. "Done!"

"How about you, Matt?" Rigor asked. "What do you plan on doing during your downtime?"

Matt shrugged. "Take out my motorcycle, go for a ride around the island, drop in on a few friends I haven't seen for a long time, maybe play a little golf. I don't know. I haven't really given it any thought."

"Well," Rigor said, "right now, my only plan is getting some sleep. Wake me when we land."

"Sounds like a good idea," Kyla agreed. She nestled into her seat. "Night, Jules."

"Night, Ky," Jules replied.

Exhausted, the team settled in for the long flight home.

———

HOURS LATER, the C-130 Hercules taxied to the CIA's private hangar at Grantley Adams International Airport.

Matt awakened to the sound of the aircraft's propellers winding down. He nudged Kyla. "We're home, hon."

Kyla stood, stretched. "Never let it be said that sleeping in those chairs is an enjoyable experience."

"Tell me about it," Jules said. She nudged Rigor's leg with her foot. "Wakey wakey, Sleeping Beauty. Up and at 'em."

"Five more minutes," Rigor replied.

Jules kicked his leg.

Rigor jumped in his seat. "Ow!" he cried. "What the hell was that?"

"Your pre-alarm going off."

Rigor shook his head. "You're a demon woman, you know that?"

Jules smiled. "Yes, I do."

Matt laughed. "Come on, tough guy. Help me offload the gear."

Rigor nodded. "Copy that."

———

MATT AND KYLA dropped Rigor and Jules at their beach house, said their goodbyes, then headed home to Matt's luxury condo in the gated community of Royal Westmoreland.

"You want a drink?" Matt asked as he dropped his bags on the vestibule floor.

"That would be great," Kyla said. "First, I'm going to take a shower. I smell like aviation fuel. Be out in a minute."

"Need a hand with anything?" Matt teased.

Kyla shook her head. "Don't even think about it, Romeo. I'm beat. Shower, scotch, sleep. That's the order of the night for me."

"So much for *my* plans."

"I promise I'll ravage you tomorrow."

Matt smiled. "Deal."

"Give me ten minutes."

"You've got it."

Matt poured the drinks and waited for Kyla to join him. He sat back in his recliner, turned on the television, and channel-surfed until he found an Oregon news station. He watched as the anchor reported on the story of the day:

POLICE HAVE NOW CLOSED *their investigation into the death of Multnomah County attorney, Jason Bettinger. The noted prose-*

cutor was found dead in his downtown law office one week ago. The cause of death has been confirmed as a self-inflicted gunshot wound to the head. He had taken his own life. Bettinger is survived by his wife, Nora, and their two children, Avril and Thomas.

"WHAT THE HELL?" Matt said.

Kyla walked into the room, towel-drying her hair. "What's wrong?"

"A friend of mine is dead," Matt replied. "I just watched the report on the news. He killed himself."

"My God, Matt. I'm so sorry. Were you two close?"

Matt nodded. "We used to be. We attended school together. Jason was a great guy." Matt shook his head. "This doesn't make sense. Jason is the last guy on the planet I can think of who would take his own life."

Matt's cell phone lay on the end table beside him. It dinged. He picked it up, read the text. "I can't believe it," he said.

"What is it?"

"It's from Nora Bettinger, Jason's wife. She wants me to call her. Thing is, I've never spoken to her before. I knew Jason before he got married and had a family."

"Call her now," Kyla said. "Put it on speaker."

Matt placed the call.

The call picked up. "Hello?"

"Nora Bettinger? This is Matt Gamble calling. I received your text."

"Oh, Matt. Thank God you called!"

"I just saw the report of Jason's death on the news," Matt

said. "I'm so sorry for your loss, Nora. Jason was a great guy. To think he took his own life..."

"That's why I reached out to you, Matt," Nora replied. "I'm not convinced that Jason killed himself. There is no way he would ever leave me or his children like that. *Never.* He loved us all too much."

"I'm sure he did." Matt paused. "Nora, would you mind telling me how you got my number? It's been years since I last spoke to Jason."

"Of course," Nora replied. "Jason rarely brought home case files from his office. I found a file sitting on his desk. It had to do with the case he was working on. I know he was concerned about it. Frankly, I'd never seen him so nervous before. Something about it was troubling him deeply. There was a slip of paper stapled to the front cover. It read 'Nora, ICOE.' Your name and number were written below it."

"ICOE," Matt said. "In case of emergency."

"That's right," Nora replied. "Jason didn't commit suicide, Matt. I know it. Someone murdered him. I want to find out who that person is and why they killed him. I think Jason was in trouble, and whatever this case is about is what got him killed. He left this note because he wanted me to reach out to you if something happened to him, so I did. Can you help us, Matt? Please?"

"Of course I will," Matt said. "Text me your address. I'll be there as soon as possible."

"Thank you, Matt. Thank you so very much."

"You're welcome, Nora," Matt replied, then ended the call.

Kyla sat quietly. "So much for piña coladas on the beach, huh?"

"You don't have to come with me," Matt replied. "I can take care of this on my own."

"Did you hear the fear in her voice, Matt?" Kyla said. "She's terrified. She needs someone to be in her corner who she can trust. I can be that person for her."

Matt nodded. "All right. I'll pack our bags. We'll leave for Oregon in the morning."

"Good."

As Matt walked to his bedroom, he thought of Jason and the good times they had shared. Now his old friend was dead, and his wife and children left alone.

If Nora was right, and someone was responsible for murdering him, he would find them and make them pay--with their life.

ALSO BY GARY WINSTON BROWN

MATT GAMBLE ACTION THRILLER SERIES

Good As Dead (Book 1)

Devil's Road (Book 2)

NOMAD (Book 3)

Savior (Coming soon)

JORDAN QUEST FBI PSYCHIC THRILLER SERIES

Intruders (Book 1)

The Sin Keeper (Book 2)

Mr. Grimm (Book 3)

Nine Lives (Book 4)

Live To Tell (Book 5)

Nemesis (Book 6)

Tiny Bones (Book 7)

Old Ghosts (Book 8)

The Bad Man (Book 9)

Two Graves (Book 10)

Ashes To Ashes (coming soon)

Jordan Quest Digital Boxset 1 (Intruders, The Sin Keeper, Mr. Grimm)

Jordan Quest Digital Boxset 2 (Nine Lives, Live To Tell, Nemesis)

Jordan Quest Digital Boxset 3 (Tiny Bones, Old Ghosts, The Bad Man)

STANDALONE THRILLERS

The Vanishing

ABOUT THE AUTHOR

Gary Winston Brown is the author of the Jordan Quest FBI Psychic Thriller series and Matt Gamble Action Thriller series. He lives outside Toronto, Canada.

If you enjoyed reading **DEVIL'S ROAD**, kindly rate and review it on Amazon!

JOIN GARY'S READERS CLUB

Want to be kept up to date on new release and preorder announcements, special offers (like signed paperback draws), and more ? It's easy. Visit my website to subscribe to my no-spam-ever newsletter and receive a free book!

GaryWinstonBrown.com

You can unsubscribe at any time, but I hope you'll stick around.

Printed in Dunstable, United Kingdom